JEAN GIONO

ENNEMONDE

TRANSLATED FROM THE FRENCH BY
Bill Johnston

archipelago books

First Archipelago Books Edition, 2021

Library of Congress Cataloging-in-Publication Data available upon request.
ISBN 9781953861122 (paperback) | ISBN 9781953861139 (ebook).

Archipelago Books
232 3rd Street #A111
Brooklyn, NY 11215
www.archipelagobooks.org

Distributed by Penguin Random House
www.penguinrandomhouse.com

Cover art by Jean Dubuffet
Cover design by Zoe Guttenplan
Interior design by Gopa & Ted2, Inc.

This book was made possible by the New York State Council on the Arts with the
support of Governor Andrew M. Cuomo and the New York State Legislature.

This work received support from the French Ministry of Foreign Affairs
and the Cultural Services of the French Embassy in the United States
through their publishing assistance program.

Funding for this book was provided by a grant from the
Carl Lesnor Family Foundation.

Archipelago Books also gratefully acknowledges the generous support
of the National Endowment for the Arts, the Lannan Foundation,
and the New York City Department of Cultural Affairs.

Printed in the United States

Ennemonde

I

JOURNEYS ARE NOT under-
taken lightly in the High Country. Farms may be five or ten miles
from their nearest neighbor. Often it would be one solitary man
traveling those miles to see another solitary man; he never does
this even once in his life. Or else it'd be a whole tribe of adults,
children, and old people setting off toward another whole tribe
of adults, children, old people – to see what? Women demolished
by repeated pregnancies, red-faced men, and crooked old folks
(and children too) – only to be looked down on by them? The
hell with that. If anyone wants to show themselves, they'll do it at
the markets. Twenty, twenty-five miles separate the villages that
neatly line the circuit formed by the road.

In the surrounding country there are beech trees, chestnuts,
sessile oaks – beeches that grow more massive the farther out

you go, sessiles that are ever more ancient; far removed from any dealings with men, there are families of birches that are lovely in summer and that disappear, white against white, in the snow. On the moors there's lavender, broom, esparto, sedge, dandelion, and then rocks, rounded rocks, as if long ago, up in these heights, great rivers used to pass through; then finally, in the great open spaces are flat rocks, resonant as bells, that repeat the slightest sound – the hop of a cricket, the patter of a mouse, the slithering of an adder, or the wind glancing off these terrestrial springboards.

The sky is often black, or at least dark blue, though giving the impression black would give – except during the blooming of the wild mignonette, whose exquisite scent is so joyful it dispels all melancholy. The time of the mignonette aside, fine weather is not cheerful in these parts; nor is it sad, it's something else; those who find it to their liking can no longer do without it. Bad weather is thoroughly seductive too, immediately assuming as it does a cosmic air. There's something galactic, extra-galactic even, in the way it behaves. It cannot rain here the way it does elsewhere – you sense that God personally sees to it; here the wind matter-of-factly takes the fate of the world in hand. The storm adapts its ways here: it doesn't flash, doesn't make any noise; simply, metallic objects begin to gleam – belt buckles, lace hooks on shoes, clasps, eyeglasses, bracelets, rings, chains. . . ; you have to mind how you go. You often find twenty, even thirty magnificent beeches struck by lightning all in a row, dead from head to foot, burned to a cinder, upright, black, bearing witness to the fact that things happen in that silence.

Dusk is more often green than red, and goes on for a very long time – so long that in the end you can't help noticing that night has fallen and that now the light is coming from the stars. In these parts the stars light your way; they're bright enough for people to recognize each other when their paths cross. It may be that you see more stars here than elsewhere; in any case, they're certainly larger, for there's something about the air – whether its purity, which is exceptional, renders the constellations more vivid or whether, as some claim, it contains some substance that acts like a magnifying glass. Naturally, no one's going to boast about having been way out in the open in the depths of night. Whenever they see it coming on, people skedaddle home before it arrives. There's a way of behaving toward this land that was perfected by our ancestors and that has produced excellent results; indeed, it's the only way: you shape yourself to it. Every accident that's been seen to happen here – and they're countless in number, including many that are strange indeed – comes from some infringement of these sorts of rules or laws.

There's nothing more straightforward for example than going from Villesèche to the Pas de Redortier in daylight; it'll take you an hour at most. The landscape isn't exactly cheerful, but it's doable; all it needs is a bit of will, or passion (if it's for hunting), or foolishness (if it's for no reason). But on a day when the clouds are low and dense, and night falls, try then! No one will chance it.

The tool that people around here have most often in their hand is a shotgun, whether it's for hunting or for, let's say, philosophical reflection; in either case, there's no solution *without* a shot being fired. The gun hangs from the stem of a wineglass that's been embedded in the wall near the chair where the man of the house sits. Whether this chair is at the table or by the fireplace, the shotgun is always within arm's reach. It's not that the region is unsafe because of a lack of police; on the contrary, even in the heyday of banditry there was never any crime up here, except for one incident in 1928, and that one was precisely about what everyone is afraid of. Everyone is afraid of loneliness. Families are no solution: at most they're collections of lonesome people who in reality are each heading in their own direction.

Families don't come together around someone; they separate as they move away from someone. Then there's metaphysics – and not the Sorbonne kind, rather the sort you have to bear in mind in confronting irredeemable solitude and the outside world. Monsieur Sartre would not be of much use here; a shotgun, on the other hand, comes in handy in many situations.

It might seem surprising that these peasants don't grasp the handles of a plow. The reason is that the peasants are shepherds. That's also what keeps them beyond (and above) technological progress. No one has yet invented a machine for minding sheep. The father, head of the family, oversees the flock; the son or sons are in charge of the small farm that in fact functions as a closed economy. People only till the acreage necessary for enough wheat, barley, potatoes, and vegetables to meet the needs of the family or the individual, and that is why so many of the peasants remain unmarried, living alone: in this way they have need of so little that they spend no more than one month a year scraping the earth.

Up until less than thirty years ago, these fiery single men had a Mahomet's Paradise for their use. It was a house on an *ubac*, or north-facing slope, the most sinister place you can imagine, which never saw sunlight even at the height of summer. A widow lived there; at the time she was sixty years old if she was a day. When some bachelor was paying her a visit, she'd hang a flag out by her door – a garden-variety blue, white, and red tricolor, the most official flag there is. In fact it had come from the town hall at Saint-C., where it had been appropriated from the stockpile kept for Bastille Day. Once the visit was over, the widow would take the flag back down. Everyone knew. There was never a problem. Right up to the day when somebody tried to change the system. A young woman from Avignon, who no doubt had the requisite skills and, by goodness, was quite the charmer, decided she'd increase productivity by home delivery of the merchandise. She made a name for herself one summer; then she vanished without a trace. Right off, a rumor went around that she'd been seen at the market in Laragne. But Laragne's a long way away. A friend of hers came asking left and right about her. He wasn't a pleasant fellow, and people stonewalled him. He tried a display of anger, but it didn't do much good. His pride must have been hurt, because – and this just isn't done – he went and told his story to the police in Sault. During the inquiry, the sighting of the young woman at Laragne and even at the market in Gap was confirmed by more than fifty witnesses whose honesty was plain to see and who, equally plainly, were not the brightest sparks. It was only three or four years later that some "stuff" turned up, which the foxes had been rummaging about in for a long time. But up in these heights there's no shortage of "stuff." The widow only shut up shop when she was over eighty. In fact, out of it all she hadn't acquired anything except the flag, which had stayed with her and which, I believe, was draped over the casket at her funeral and afterwards put up on her grave, where the wind and the rain eventually reduced it to tatters, though before that happened I managed to see it with my own eyes.

The women in these parts have no shape; they're bundles of low-quality fabrics. It's not for want of a desire to look good; quite the opposite, on that front they're more than likely to vie with each other. But the market stallholders sell peasant snobbery more than quality merchandise. The women no longer go in for spotted fabrics, or for the jet black that looked so lovely on their forebears; they want modern designs. And that's what they get. The patterns suit them like an apron on a pig, in colors that would make even an architect scream (which is no small feat). But you have to let people know you've got money. To the point that if you see someone dressed tastefully, looking like a princess among all those lumpy women, you can bet your bottom dollar she's poor and she's ashamed. Sometimes really old women cause a stir. Once they pass the age when they can be knocked up, their body is renewed; even those who remain on the plump side become shapely, while the skinny ones take on a true nobility. That's also a time when they have very little money, and so they go back to their old cotton prints. In each family, then, there is something of beauty (which is loathed).

The young women, while they're still maidens, possess a fruit-like beauty; then the beauty bursts, and fragments of it can be seen in their children. Truly nothing remains of these women's former state. Some Venuses turn into fearsome monsters; almost all of them have seventeenth-century mouths, toothless or, even worse, with a handful of loose teeth on which they suck. It's pretty ghastly. But their simple-minded appearance shouldn't be taken at face value. Almost all of them are commanding women. With their backs to the wall they achieve wonders. People still remember Ennemonde Girard.

She'd been born a Martin, and had spent all the flower of her youth at Le Gour des Oules in the narrow little valley that separates the mountains of Lure and Ventoux. She wanted to be a schoolteacher, but she failed the entrance exam to the École Normale or teacher training college. She went back to the farm and minded the sheep. On the ubacs near Croix de l'Homme

Mort Pass she started meeting once a week with a young man from Séderon who used to cross the mountain with cartloads of wood destined for the preserve factories of Apt and the bakeries in the Calavon valley. The First World War was just coming to an end. At that time ovens were still fired with bundles of white oak. The boy, Honoré Girard, though he claimed to be from Séderon, where his parents had indeed settled, originally came from Chamoune and in fact from Reychasset. In other words, from what's known around here as the tiger wilds, a maze of small dark valleys where back in the day the most uncompromising of the heretics had taken refuge. Right up until 1950 or so, pastors responsible for the souls of the local communities (which were extremely small) would protest vehemently against Protestantism itself and impose the most strenuous spiritual gymnastics on their flocks. Generally speaking, people are on their guard against trapeze artists of that ilk. But try finding fault with blue eyes, a fine aquiline nose, a nicely put together face, a slender body, and a way of talking enriched by the Old Testament, when you've failed your entrance exam to the teacher training college! Every Friday, around three o'clock Ennemonde would lead her flock up toward the road where Honoré Girard would stop his carts.

In spite of the dense woods and the pretty groves of broom, Ennemonde married in white. The young couple began farming at a *jas*, or sheep shelter, high up on the side of Pendu Hill six miles from Ferrassières. It was a good spot, capable of supporting two hundred sheep. They started with twenty ewes, cleared their fifteen acres, and from the second year their livelihood was secure.

Right from the beginning Honoré made his wife wear a nightshirt with a hole in it. This long garment of coarse fabric allows one to make babies without any reprehensible flourishes. By this somewhat vexing procedure she had five children in four and a half years, then one a year, up to thirteen. She lost twenty or so teeth; in the end she prized out the last two with the point of a knife. She was obese, with massive buttocks; her husband's belt was supposedly too small to go around the base of her thigh; on the other hand, her bust grew flatter. But she still had her lovely hair of the glossiest black (she wasn't yet forty years old) and, wonder of wonders, ankles of an exceptional fineness.

They may not have had a lot of money, but they'd bought the jas (from a count who lived in Carpentras), leased pastureland, and Honoré's flock, numbering almost three hundred head, was famous. Buyers would always visit him first, before anyone else.

Life was good, despite the nightshirt with the hole, on which Honoré wouldn't budge. He was fond enough of good meat, and they ate well throughout the winter. He never learned what decent wine is, but that was an ignorance shared by the entire region; like everyone else he enjoyed a bottle of the vinegary stuff from Gignac. For want of other options, Ennemonde had become an excellent cook; she put all her heart into it. She cooked anything: thrushes, plovers, young boars, hares. They killed two pigs each year, one in the fall, one in spring, and someone in the know might have been able to predict a certain future if they'd seen the sensual delight with which Ennemonde ground up by hand the mixture of chopped liver and fat from the family butchering.

Honoré claimed that all this was in the Bible. But something happened that was not to be found in the Good Book. Honoré began to shrink. This is an expression used in these parts for a rather common phenomenon. When a man (or a woman) no longer has sufficient curiosity about the natural world, they take refuge in the unusual. This unusualness can sometimes be thoroughly banal: they stop getting undressed, for instance, or speaking, or walking; they stop going to such and such a town or such and such market; they stop seeing anyone; at times it can be something as silly as not putting their hands in their pockets anymore, or no longer wiping their eyeglasses, or taking off their hat. This is done, I imagine, in the hope that a world lacking a particular thing, whatever it is, will be a different world. And in fact it must work, since people who shrink in this way never go back to their normal size. The unusual isn't restricted to banalities, though, and some folks have shrunk in such a manner as to edge their way into a fantastical world. Numa Pellisson, for instance, spent two years living in a village of crows at the top of a sixty-foot beech tree. He ate eggs from the nests, and to quench his thirst in the summer he drank the blood of a bird. He died up there, and in the end the feathered creatures ate him. But let's come back to Honoré.

His shrinking was not that of a great nobleman, but it was extremely troublesome all the same: he decided never to sell anything ever again, neither ewes, nor lambs, nor rams. The flock multiplied beyond measure, whereas the pasturage stayed the same size. The lambs became scrawny, the ewes died. Those that survived were skin and bones. Buyers, rebuffed whenever they appeared, eventually stopped going anywhere near the ill-fated flock. Ennemonde, who herself was deprived of her necessities, began to find her coffee a little bitter. She leaped into action at once. She made sure the first six children, the oldest ones, were on her side. That part was easy. In collusion with them she took possession of the shotgun. Honoré was immediately relegated to second, even fifth place: the fifth wheel on the wagon. Ennemonde was smart enough to leave him the wherewithal to satisfy his obsession: twenty animals which she let him keep. But twenty, not twenty-one, to the point that she would have the lambs they produced. She took charge of the rest masterfully, the gun slung on her shoulder, with her two oldest sons, who at the time were fifteen and fourteen respectively. Which is to say, were men. She was swiftly and unanimously acknowledged as the *patronne*. It's at this point that her story intersects with that of Clef-des-coeurs, as we'll see when it's time to speak of that individual.

The rest is commonplace and has no story attached. Honoré was killed a few years later by a kick from a mule. At least that's what people surmised, and very likely it was true. He owned one that was extremely stubborn. They found his body at the feet of the creature in the stable; his head was smashed in, and the mark left by the iron shoe was clear as day. What more could you ask for?

In these parts, men are not handsome in old age. They last a long time – it's not unusual to meet someone who's over ninety years old; many approach a hundred – but they go bad from the age of eighty. The ones who up till that moment have kept their looks, and sometimes even seem as if they're on their way to acquiring a new elegance, collapse and shrivel up, prey to worms before their death, which now becomes no more than a formality required by law. They could be buried without risk (to someone's conscience) before that formality is completed. Alas, such a thing is not permitted. Their bones last a long time, but their souls do not. This is so because the men are deprived of their hearts early: some have lost them by the age of ten, others never had one from the moment they were born. The best of them rid themselves of that useless muscle around the age of twenty-five. People who are merely passing through, or only know the region slightly, don't notice; in most cases the old men cover it up, right until the day when it becomes clear that for them the heart was not needed. The day when it is, we find ourselves facing slabs of stone.

They're civilized people, of course. Much more civilized, in fact, than other peasants or other recluses; and above all they possess a practical intelligence far more acute than that of folks in the Low Country. With strangers – and they consider anyone a stranger who hasn't lived up in the heights for centuries – they're polite, friendly, kind, likable, helpful. The point is that they don't have any real relationship with strangers. They treat them the way people treat children – though not their own children; their own children aren't strangers. They permit a stranger certain liberties, though they'll fire an abrupt warning shot should the need arise. With their peers they give no advance notice; they act at once, without hesitation and without heart.

This realist approach at first glance seems at odds with the fact that they inhabit a land where life can only sustain itself with a constant supply of unreality (as we shall see). But reality pushed to an extreme meets back up again with unreality. To face things full on is to accept their magic; in any case, not to argue with it.

Around here, the life people lead doesn't allow them to treat others with kid gloves. The Dianas of Montemayor, all those Faithful Shepherds, the Astrées, and the Marie-Antoinettes have spread the image of pastoral sheepfolds as havens of peace. Who could be gentler, it's said, than those who live day to day with animals that the wisdom of nations has taken as the epitome of mildness: gentle as a sheep? Sheep aren't gentle, they're stupid. Sustained contact with stupidity means that people inhabit a bizarre world. Rams are aggressive animals; ewes come to us in a direct line from the bestiality trials of the Middle Ages. The people in these parts live every day alongside that stupidity, that aggression, that unhealthy temptation God has created, in utter solitude.

For the common run of mortals, a shepherd is someone who dreams as he leans on his crook. Sure he dreams – what else do you expect him to do? – but in his situation he's tempted at every moment to carry out those dreams, without any major hindrance. He only needs to set aside certain laws, certain precepts, certain customs. That's quickly done. What could be more delicious than bypassing laws and ridiculing customs? Especially when the life you lead is hard: wind, cold, snow, rain, solitude, fear – not the fear we all know, that seizes us fiercely and eventually passes, but a local kind of fear that never ends.

God preserve us from shepherds' dreams! Genghis Khan was a shepherd. The eye of the sheep is an opening through which you can sneak a look at the voluptuous antics of stupidity. Afterward, you're not going to raze Samarkand, or build pyramids of thousands of severed heads on the banks of the Oxus. But the fact is you're alone. There's no lack of desire; it's all too present. So you start to dream about what you might be able to do in your little part of the country: there are markets, there are holidays, there are families. Sometimes you manage to do some pretty nice things, sometimes you don't; circumstances don't always play along. At times you have to deal with individuals who put up a fight, families that don't allow themselves to be wiped away, children who grow up quickly; with adversaries who have also looked into the eye of the sheep. The important thing isn't to win but to always have at hand the means for continuing the game, such that families and communities remain, outwardly at least, intact.

One day, up on the Négron Pass a bloodstained corduroy jacket is found. It's not just bloodstained, and horribly so – there are strips of flesh attached – but it's torn to pieces and chewed up as if a tiger's been at it. Questions are asked all around. No one recognizes the jacket. More questions: has anyone disappeared – no. So then, the jacket belongs to some offcomer. Screw him! Everyone loses interest. The gendarmes make three more turns then off they go.

It was April. The serviceberries were in bloom in the hollows; up on the heights the foxtail grass was starting to turn red. The ubacs oozed water into the streams. In the High Country this is the season of rumors. The grass itself seems to buzz with them. When the wind stops blowing, what follows is not silence but a thousand muffled sounds. There's no birdsong: the thrushes, quail, plovers, robins, chickadees, and so on are still down below in the valleys; only the one-note cry of the eagles can be heard in a brief round toward four in the afternoon. The ravens and crows are in their nests.

Just that year, the Richards (of Saumane) had divided their flock in two and entrusted one half to Siméon, their eldest. He was a boy of fourteen, but he had already looked into the eye of the sheep. One afternoon, on his pasture, at least ten miles from the Négron, he was on a ridge overlooking the extensive ubacs that drop almost vertically toward the Jabron, when he heard a strange commotion in the thickets of white oak and holly that carpet the slopes. The noise was accompanied by a rustle of dry leaves as if a large creature were passing by. There are often wild boars in the neighborhood. He took his shotgun and waited.

Nothing came except the night. Siméon went back to his jas, which was half a mile or so away. He brought his sheep in and barricaded himself inside with them. Things looked a bit dubious to him. The Richards' farm was twelve miles away. But for a few months now Siméon had had a shotgun with an automatic ejector, and he was in no danger of being cowed by the dubiousness of events. He loaded both barrels with cartridges for big game and lay down near the door.

He was woken in the middle of the night by a ferocious smell (it stank of the devil!) and also by his sheepdog, which was pressing itself against him for comfort, trembling. Yet the dog was a plucky animal that didn't scare easily. The stench was terrible. Siméon also heard some creature breathing outside the door, then scratching against it. Don't move, don't open the door; stay calm. And that's what the shepherd boy did.

He wasn't proud of himself in the morning! But the flock had to be let out. Something of the awful odor still lingered. If you couldn't rely on a shotgun with an automatic ejector, though, what could you rely on? Let's put a brave face on it! He opened the door. He could tell something had been going on in the little area where the drinking troughs and the salt feeders were, and the sheep knew it too, because they refused to go lick the salt. But of a morning there aren't any giants or lions; everything is regular size, and things that are regular size are dealt with in a regular way, using a shotgun with an automatic ejector, especially one with advanced choking to the left and advanced semi-choking to the right, and with Hercules steel barrels.

He killed the horrible thing a little before midday. By then the sun was heavy in the sky; the flock, which had already eaten its fill, was moving at a snail's pace because of the heat. But since leaving the shelter, the sheepdog's ears had been pricked and it had kept its eye firmly on its master, who, gun in hand, had kept his eye firmly on the dog. Both were on the qui vive. All at once the dog made a little sound – just enough to call its master's attention, so as not to alarm the sheep, since this had nothing to do with them. Siméon saw some beast come out from behind a pile of rocks. He let loose with both barrels, without a second thought, at the same time saying to himself: "It looks like two dogs tied together. But what's that they're pulling between them?" And in fact it was two dogs attached to a corpse that they'd been dragging around for two days.

Siméon put his flock back in the shelter and ran to tell the other shepherds who were grazing their animals a few miles farther down the mountain. The police came up. They all discussed what had happened, or more precisely, what might have happened.

They could have searched for a hundred years and more. Who would have thought to connect the bloody jacket found on the Négron Pass with Jules Dupuis, known as Wagtail? The Dupuis are far from being offcomers; there are Dupuis girls in nine families out of ten; there are Dupuis known as Sniffler,

Dupuis known as No-Work, Dupuis known as Melchior, Dupuis known as Automobile, Ironhead Dupuis, Anvil Dupuis, and this Dupuis, who was known as Wagtail (a kind of bird). No one could have reported his disappearance since he lived alone like a miser in a hollow that was dark as a cauldron, on an ubac toward Pompe, where no one ever goes. Who could know if he was there or if he wasn't; and if he wasn't, who could tell if he'd disappeared or if he'd just gone to buy supplies in Omergues or Séderon, in Montfroc, or even as far away as Châteauneuf-Miravail.

The fact is, he never went anywhere without his two dogs chained to his belt. He started doing this after a brawl he'd gotten into with a guy named Martin from Montbrun. And here we come back toward Ennemonde Girard, because this Martin was her first cousin and had even been something of a boyfriend of hers when she still had hopes for teacher training college. Later on we may well see the same Martin make a pretty penny; but a short while after his kissing-cousins episode with Ennemonde, he had a run-in with the law. I say the law, not the police. Usually, around here the local gendarmes can handle things, whereas for this guy people came from a long way away, from Digne, even Marseille I believe. I don't exactly know what it was all about;

there was talk of his place being searched, mention of parcels being stolen from the mail; I'm not really sure on the details, and besides, they let him go.

He ran a service between Montbrun and Sisteron in a rickety old bus, and it was because of an argument in the bus that he got into a fight with Wagtail Dupuis. It happened on the Macuègne Pass above Barret. The two men, who were alone in the vehicle, got out and went at it in the road. Wagtail got the upper hand, and Martin said he'd "do him in" the next chance he got. Hence the two dogs.

But it might not have been only about that, the business with the dogs. At this point, Monsieur Fouillerot entered the picture. That meant something. Monsieur Fouillerot even went to the trouble of paying a visit to the police station in person. He wanted to know, first, if they were sure the body really was that of Wagtail Dupuis. They were. The head was still missing; it had gotten separated while the dogs had been trailing around up on the heights. The police were looking for it. But the dogs were Wagtail's dogs, the belt they'd been attached to was Wagtail's, and so the body around which the belt was fastened had a very good chance of being his.

Then Fouillerot, that is to say Monsieur Fouillerot, announced that Jules Dupuis, known as Wagtail, had owned more than a million in Treasury bills. This was 1934. Talk of a shock! They had to start again at square one, after they'd already figured everything out: Wagtail had gone to Omergues – that part had been established, he'd been seen. He'd spent the whole day knocking it back, mixing white and red, that had been established too, they'd identified people he'd been drinking with. Late in the evening he'd decided to go back up to his place; he'd been caught unawares by the cold; he'd died; afterwards his dogs had dragged him around. As if Wagtail could be taken unawares by anything! Even when he was three sheets to the wind! But an autopsy's an autopsy, and facts are facts. It's just that a million, that's a fact too. So where was it, the million?

First of all though, who was Fouillerot, Monsieur Fouillerot? Here too there was something solid to go on. Fouillerot was a former bailiff who'd exercised his talents over toward Draguignan. After making his fortune (in a modest kind of way) he'd come back to the region, because he was from here. He'd bought a little property a few miles from Le Revest, and after two or three years of – well, of conversations, inquiries, visits to cafés –

he'd set up in business lending money left and right, first at low rates of annual interest, then at high rates, then at high rates of annual interest and with monthly payments. At times it came in handy for people. He was also a bank agent, and as such he cashed bank drafts and invested in stocks and shares for others. That was how he knew about Wagtail's fortune in Treasury bills. He was the one who'd sold him the bills, which were guaranteed by the government. He was proud of having done it.

They started by going through Wagtail's home with a fine-tooth comb. Now that was a job for a young girl! They found rats, moldy fox skins, old cheeses, but also an Olibet cookie tin containing forty gold coins. The million seemed within reach. After that, though, they didn't find anything else. At the same time, who knows if the discovery of the gold coins hadn't spurred other people? They even had to leave a gendarme to keep an eye on the place at night.

Fouillerot, or rather Monsieur Fouillerot, suggested that Wagtail must have carried his fortune on his person at all times. He explained that the bills were in the form of large-denomination notes that could very easily be kept in a jacket or pants pocket, or a specially made pouch. Thoughts turned abruptly to the jacket found on the Négron Pass. In fact, thoughts turned to many things. To the jacket, to Martin, to Siméon, and to the idea of exhuming Wagtail.

There was nothing in the jacket, which was at the police station. But perhaps someone had gone through it before. Martin? No, he'd been home with a broken leg for the last three weeks. Siméon? No. You only needed to look at the kid: he was capable of killing a monster, but not of laying hands on a rotting cadaver. Besides, why would he have? Aside from Fouillerot, no one knew about the million.

So there! It was quite something! Though when all was said and done, it wasn't, since Fouillerot had spoken, and on top of that he'd just given the police the numbers of the Treasury bills, which meant they could now be stopped. And by the way, what was a million to Monsieur Fouillerot when the whole of the High Country was his milch cow?

Time passes, summer arrives, storms break out, rain falls, animals multiply, foxes, badgers, martens, weasels (I think about Wagtail's head, which still hasn't been found), and every kind of rodent from squirrels to rats to shrews: not much chance that a Treasury bill, even a large-denomination one, could withstand all that. By now only the Melchior Dupuis still chew on that million from time to time; for everyone else it's lost its flavor.

Plus, people say, who knows? Maybe there was no million. That Fouillerot always plays a queer game; who can tell if this time too he's not leading everyone up the garden path?

Up till now it's been the surface of the culture that's been seen. Everything seems to be happening more or less like it does in the Low Country, or anywhere else for that matter. There are gendarmes, there are even the numbers of the Treasury bills, and they can be stopped, the way it'd be done in Paris or in Romorantin. There's even an autopsy, a rudimentary one I'll admit, since it's performed by a local doctor unaccustomed to police procedures. It proves impossible to determine the day, and all the more the exact hour, of death. But could anyone have done that? Wagtail is something of a mess after being hauled through the bushes by the big hounds that were tethered to his fate.

In the end we have the Melchior Dupuis claiming they're distantly related and asking for the estate, at least the forty gold louis (of which the government will anyway take thirty-nine). Wagtail is buried (twice). The dogs are buried. Things resume their usual course.

At some point during this History and Geography of the High Country, an opportunity may arise to sneak a glance at the color of the cards, their other side, which no longer bears any image of culture. The game will certainly not be revealed in its entirety, that's not to be expected; but Ennemonde, the Melchior Dupuis, this Fouillerot fellow, perhaps even the widow with the flag – there's material here for a research project, and whoever searches finds (though not always what they're looking for, especially around here). Also, they're not the only ones involved; there are those who are going to cross their path, and those who've already crossed it and retrace their steps, or continue on. What's sure is that it won't be a matter of conversations but of actions: in these parts, people talk little and act a lot. They look like they're asleep or daydreaming, leaning on a walking stick, or moving along very slowly, but in the end they strike a heck of a light and send all kinds of sparks flying.

On the subject of heart (or lack thereof, which we were speaking of a moment ago), there are two characters worth looking at. First there's Wagtail himself; then there's young Siméon. At the moment of his death Wagtail was sixty-nine – sixty-nine years and three months, to be precise. The million had amazed everyone because the word itself does that. But Wagtail could have had a million; if he'd sold his whole stock of lavender essence, he could even have had more. He sold a pretty large part of it, his stock that is, to a broker from Grasse who had gotten himself introduced; the part he hadn't sold was not found. But take note: there's the government, which took thirty-nine gold louis out of forty; the Melchiors have no wish to go on enriching the tax man at such a rate, so what was found and what was not found was as clear as mud, because how can you keep an eye on seals on the ubacs of Pompe, where any little thing – a frost, a thaw – can make the wax crack, where the wind can break down doors, where a whole day's journey by foot is needed to go check on things. Very well – this has been an aside to lend substance to the million that was good for nothing in the ubacs. Let's come back to Wagtail.

Sixty-nine years old. He'd never been a giant: five foot four at his fullest glory. It had been ten years since he'd begun living with two dogs chained to his belt. At first he'd had two big reddish-brown ones. One of them died; then he had a reddish-brown one and a black one. The ones that had dragged him around, and eaten part of his innards, were two large German shepherds. For ten years Wagtail had walked about, had slept, attached to two dogs. When he went for a drink, the dogs would lie down next to him. With a single word – even less, with a click of his tongue – he could launch them at anyone's throat. What had he been so afraid of to arrive at such a state of affairs? Being robbed?

No – the shotgun he, like everyone else, carried was more than enough to protect him from robbery. He wasn't afraid of Martin or of Montbrun; it came out later that after they'd gotten into that barney with each other they'd become firm friends, as often happens, and that sometimes they'd even go together (along with the two dogs) for a little evening of dissoluteness at the home of the widow with the flag, who sold wine under the counter.

The locations people around here have for centuries chosen for their houses always come as a surprise to outsiders. They're never built in front of a lovely view, whereas places called "Belle Vue" (there are many of them) are always abandoned. Visitors think they tuck their dwellings at the very bottoms of valleys, and in the darkest spots, and sometimes in places the sun never reaches, so as to shelter from the wind. Yet, once you get to know the folks around here a little, you find out that they're crazy about the wind, that they'd pay to have some wind. In fact they don't need to pay: they have it already, reliably, constantly. So it's not because of the wind that they hide themselves away; it's so that, insofar as they're able, they can do away with anything that exceeds them. And when I say exceeds, I'm talking about size.

When they're at home, whether they're looking out the window, or standing against their walls, everything is human height, even the tallest beech trees, which they can always climb and, if need be, live in, as was the case with the famous Numa Pellisson. So then, no problems of consciousness. They have a sense of themselves. This is no longer the case when they're up in the high places; and they have to go up there thousands of times in their life, often early in the morning – like Siméon, for example, who's only fourteen years old – and sometimes they have to go up for a long time.

As you climb higher, the toughest oaks and the tallest beeches disappear after dropping all the way to your feet. There's a moment when the crowns of the trees touch the soles of your shoes; now the horizon unfurls. And Christendom fades away. Because God made enemies, he made this landscape, they say. That which destroys the hearts of humans is never terrible but, on the contrary, gladly tolerates calm and beauty. From Mount Viso, which is to say from Italy, all the way to Gerbier de Joncs and even, beyond that, to the dark bluffs of the Margeride, which is to say as far as Auvergne; and from Mont Blanc, which can be seen from far up in the North like a hazy looking glass, as far as Mount Sainte-Victoire, which sails due south in full rigging, and even, via the gap that separates Sainte-Victoire from Mount Apollon, all the way to the sea, whose lovely foaming roundness can be seen – these are the two diameters. Around the circumference of the circle, moving from the east and passing via the south: first, the High Alps of the Briançon region – Pelvoux with its snow and its Écrins, then Queyras and Viso – before which rise the Alps around Gap, the Dauphiné d'Orcières, then, a little farther forward, the Alps of Digne and of Barcelonnette, which they call the Low Alps, contrary to all reality. The latter are linked to closer massifs, while the high peaks fly away toward the Italian border: Mount Castellane, the Mourre de Chanier, and Aiguines Mountain, which drops gently all the way to the plateaus of the Haut-Var. That, in turn, is seen spreading the red shimmer of its great oak forests in winter, and in summer the winey blue of its deep oceans. Finally two-headed Mount Apollon emerges, and a sheer cliff that the misinformed take for Sainte-Victoire and which in fact is Sainte-Baume, then Sainte-Victoire; but in the meantime, above the fields of Pourrières where the Cimbri and the Teutons were crushed, the sea has been glimpsed. From those parts, in the area between the south and the west, where in the afternoons a sort of luminous dust billows, the sky strives to touch the low lands of the Crau, the Camargue, and the marshes of the Gulf of Lion. On this side, then, there's no trace of a mountain, but often, at the moment you least expect it, in calm, fine weather for instance, a strange color is seen to rise. It's a kind of black in which flecks of light seem to be quivering. At times you could imagine that the Andes or the Himalayas had loomed up with their shadows; at other moments it might be the sea rearing against a wall; in reality, it's light devouring itself and, having done so, leaving in its place an abyss that is not even cosmic. This ferocity of light comes from the ceaseless shimmer of the choppy sea off Port-Saint-Louis-du-Rhône and Saintes-Maries, magnified by the vast lens of the Vaccarès Lagoon and the dazzling vapors drawn by the sun from the lands kissed by the Rhône. The scrublands of Nîmes cannot find a way out of this inferno. They can only be made out in the morning, when the sun is behind you. At such moments, in springtime the rock-rose flowers make them look as if they're incrusted with salt. On the outskirts of these lands of light, the rustic mountains of the Lozère begin to rise: the Branoux which overlooks Alès; the Aigoual leaning against the Causse Noir; the Méjean towering over Florac; the Lozère overlooking Mende; and far in the distance, the Aubrac, which from here looks like a pool of gilded lichen. It's in those mountains that, in summer, the sun sets. But when it drops down upon them it obliterates them, wipes them out, and it only lights up its fireworks farther to the north: in the

Auvergne, the mountains of Mutat, the Margeride that remains acid green all summer, despite how far away it is; the mountains of Allègre, of the Chaise-Dieu, the Pilat; then suddenly, after the Pilat, a scrap of horizon in which there is nothing – that's the valley through which the Rhône descends. After that, you have to look way up high to see the glimmer of Mont Blanc; then the mountains of the Dauphiné come and attach themselves to those of Briançon and the circle of the spike trap is closed.

If, from the summit of the Gondran which overlooks Montgenèvre, you take a few steps in the direction of the Infernet, then in the distance, toward Marseille, between the peaks of Embrun and Queyras, you can see a white ridge: that's the High Country. If, from Toulon, you're heading toward the valley of the Gapeau and you take the road from Solliès-Pont to Brignoles, once you round the massif of Sainte-Baume and you're at the crossroads of the Saint-Maximan road, go another twenty yards or so to the right of the road, toward a splendid cherry tree, and, looking northward, you see a little white triangle in the sky: that's the High Country. It can be seen from the road from Saint-Flour to Le Puy, right where you begin the descent into Langeac, a short ways after Pinols; it's to the east, like a cloud. On the other hand, if you're coming from Paris by car or on the train, you'll never see it: after Valence it'll be hidden by the mountains of the Drôme, after Orange concealed by the Ventoux, after Avignon obliterated by the light.

Summer and winter, from all these distant vantage points it appears white. In the winter, of course, that's from the snow. But winter is not the season to fear most in the High Country. The summer claims many more victims here. It's wrong to imagine that Jesus Christ has changed everything; up here, such a fact is plain. The snow is nothing, even when it's piled by the wind into drifts thirty feet deep, even when in its storms it swallows up fathers of families on their way back from buying bread for the week. A man born in these parts, raised in these forests, pursuing his occupation in these heights, is oblivious to the Christian hell. The notion of sin is utterly at odds with the wind rose. If the man wishes to live he has to sin, every day, every hour, and even to invent new sins a thousand times more mortal than the famous ones known to be so. He has to create a personal arsenal of them, mark them with his initials, employ them in his own way, which is the only way they can be utilized properly and with perfect effectiveness. The New Testament agrees with no one; the Old Testament with some people, sometimes; but what accords with everyone is the sense (which has no name in any language) that nothing is dust. From that point, only individuals are possible, and their hearts, which are useless, or which get in the way like the Amazon's breast. People remove their own very early, well before finishing elementary school.

The summer glitters and is short. It breaks clear of the spring in five days, flourishes in twenty, convulses in ten, and then it's autumn. By each jas there's a cherry tree; some were planted, many grew by themselves. They have nothing in common with the cherry trees of the plains or the valleys. Generally this cherry tree is very low with a huge trunk, oozing golden gobs from all the scars on its bark. Its branches, underdeveloped because of the winds with which it is perpetually in open conflict, bear small leaves and tiny fruits little bigger than the red currants that ripen at the end of July. At that point, the season has only just brushed off the spring; its white powder is still suspended in the morning light, but already, suddenly the middays are oppressive, and the evenings drag on endlessly in red until the first star finally appears. The air has all at once become edible. Only those who have breathed it can understand the merit of this term. The lungs become an instrument of cognition. It's not a matter of smell, or freshness, but of chemical quality (like that of jugged hare). For a very long moment it seems that all movement has become useless, and so there is no more sound. From the tiniest insect to the largest quadruped, nothing moves unless it's absolutely necessary: mere breathing is enough; this breathing brings an unparalleled joy that satisfies even the insatiable curiosity of humans. Yes indeed, it really does seem as if the very appetite for knowing has been sated purely by the act of filling oneself with air. The bees are the first to pull themselves together and realize that, on the contrary, they need to get a move on; then the birds: first the thick-billed hawfinches with their graceless, monotonous song, feeding on seeds and the bastard esparto grass that covers the steppe; the thin-billed birds, carnivorous and cruel, begin by describing arabesques as they explore the sky from ground level to heights where the lark is already quivering, and then they express themselves in brief, febrile songs like cries; then finally the weighty birds of prey rise from the grass where they have been sleeping.

It's a carrion season. Sheep are quickly driven wild in the bright mornings. Bees track tawny little reptile-like beasts – ferrets, stoats, weasels, martens – in hopes of coming by some freshly spilled blood or something rotten, from which, joyfully, they make their sugar. They stack their hundredweights of black sulfur-scented honey in the trunks of dead trees. It's so heavy that often the wood of these trees, dried by the sun and the winds, shatters and the honey spills, while the fury of millions of bees sets the sky ablaze. Events of this kind are not rare; they create an emptiness around them. In 1927 the oldest Bernard, who hadn't gotten out in time, was held prisoner in his own jas for over a week. You can't keep sheep shut in without food for a week. On the second day, the oldest Bernard (Kléber) managed to free his flock. Sheep are not particularly afraid of bee stings, except on the muzzle, but when that happens they secrete an acidic mucus that protects them; the bees, on the other hand, get trapped in the fleece. Kléber knew this and was somewhat counting on it. The flock carried off a good number of the warriors, but some that remained went back and forth, as it were, and brought reinforcements. The oldest Bernard can't talk about it even now without trembling. He felt himself overpowered – him, a guy who at that time already weighed a good two hundred pounds – and there was nothing he could do about it. And by the way, he wasn't rescued by anyone. When the Bernards saw their sheep turn up at their place, they realized what had happened, but what could be done? They tried to make it up to the jas, but after they'd gone half a mile, right where you pass beyond the ridge, they heard the humming on the other side and saw, yonder in front of them, the building that had lost its angles and its shape and had become nothing but a ball of bees. There were in fact one or two beekeepers in those parts, even one who, so he claimed, knew how to charm the bees and had posed for a photograph with a swarm clinging to his cheeks and hanging from his chin like a beard. But this was too much for him. He couldn't believe his eyes, he said, but he preferred to believe them than to take a closer look. Someone thought of the flamethrowers they use in the army, and the town hall called Digne, which called Avignon, but they didn't have any flamethrowers; the works department at Avignon suggested bringing in firefighters. To do what? What could they fight with, in this land where water is rarer than wine? All the more because shooting water at bees (at these bees) was. . . I've too much respect for you to finish. Yet they couldn't leave the oldest Bernard in this situation, could they? They did though. Finally, four or five days later, one morning he arrived home, shaking like a leaf. What had happened? He had no idea. All he could say was that, in contrast with the previous nights, last night the incessant pattering against the windows had ceased, as had the buzzing that kept up in the chimney despite the raging fire he'd maintained without a break. He went to take a look; the window panes were clear, and he could "see the stars again." Still, he remained on his guard. When daylight came, he saw that the siege had been lifted. He opened the door and threw a few pebbles into the grass, poised to close up again if it was an ambush. No, they'd left. He ran for the valley.

He wasn't delivered, then; the bees had delivered him, left him to his sorry fate. His self-esteem remained hurt, like someone who has experienced contempt. Nor could he understand why no one had come to his aid. His father said it was because he didn't want to understand. Yes in fact, he did want to. He wasn't some minor member of the family. He was the eldest, and he wanted to know why he'd been abandoned. It did no good to repeat to him that it wasn't a matter of knowing but of understanding, and in order to understand, he needed to put himself in their place. He couldn't be made to admit that his place had not been the worst possible one.

When people chat with the oldest Bernard these days, or when they're discussing business with him, they always have to be wary; he sometimes answers back in ways that are hard to take. He's married, he even has a pretty little daughter. His gaze is not open; you sense that he's weighing you up mentally, and calculating. What can he be calculating?

As for him, the bees that were laying siege must have received the order to abandon him. They're often seen to be receiving orders. They're not furious all the time. They're never particularly proper, but you can get on fine with them so long as you don't allow yourself to be overfamiliar and if you always cede territory to them. Toward Larrau there are a couple dozen dead oaks; these are very big trees that, one after another, have been struck by lightning over the course of the last thirty years. To begin with, bit by bit they lost their top branches, then their bark came off and they were left there white as ivory. When you go up to them, you're amazed to hear them all a-murmur despite what's happened to them. Stop at once: those are bees. The greatest concentration of wild bees in the entire region. In the sixteenth century there was something similar, perhaps on an even grander scale, thirty miles west of here at the entrance to the gorges of the Nesque River at the place known today as Rock of Wax.

The trunks are easily between seven and ten feet in circumference, twenty or twenty-five feet high, and stuffed to the brim with black honey that smells slightly of sulfur, as well as with numberless battalions, republics, and other mass organizations. From here political commando units fly out with the goal of disrupting, corrupting, seducing, bribing, and ultimately leading away the peaceful inhabitants of the bourgeois hives that are kept at some of the farms. These expeditions can be seen racing across the steppe like pale gray mist. It's of course vital to keep out of their way, but if for some reason they can't be avoided, there's little risk. The expeditions are purely political in nature and are likely made up of orators rather than warriors. If you do find yourself face to face with such a group, all you need to do is not run away and not wave your arms about; if you stand still, there's no danger.

The same cannot be said of the fringes of the shattered forest. Around their metropolis the bees have established a frontier that should not be crossed. It's air within air, but if you wish to know it, that's easily done: cross it. Cross it, let's be clear, with the greatest possible caution, one step at a time, ready to turn back at the least sign, which will not be late in coming: the moment you've passed the designated line, on the other side of which the bees regard you as being on their turf, the warriors come streaming out. Turn about, go back where you belong, they won't pursue you; they hover for a while at the limit of their territory; they wait; if you don't push it, they head back to barracks, one platoon after another. Try it ten times; ten times they'll start up again exactly the same.

The furious droning of these warriors when they charge is

terrifying. It's like the sound of thunder; I mean that it's of the same quality. It simultaneously brings the same pleasure to the ear and the same unease to the heart. Now that I think about it, it's much more alarming than the noise of thunder. Like thunder, it's cosmic, and it's simply produced by the insects rubbing their bellies to express their anger. Thus Zeus and the god of Abraham are no more deeply rooted in the world than this pale little creature: all it takes is for it to be a million or two strong and to scratch its belly with nails a tenth of a millimeter long for its wrath to be on the scale of infinite space. There's also the god of Cromwell: he withstands the comparison.

Another peculiarity of the summer is that it's the breeding ground of the passions. There is no hatred, no ambition, no jealousy, no love that could fail to do battle during this short fragile month. Loving is only there for memory's sake; for it, the matter is straightforward and quickly settled: girls conceive in August (and married women in January). These conceptions often arise not from a free giving of oneself, but a sort of ram-and-ewe coupling. There are exceptions: one of the Rupert-Calicot wives conceived in August, even though she had long rounded the stormy cape: it was her fourth child. Her husband seemed to regard it all as completely normal. He didn't fool anyone. The son that was subsequently born has never been treated the same as his brothers and sisters. People are still wondering. From time to time someone thinks: maybe so-and-so? And for six months they speculate and find a resemblance. Then they can't see it any longer, and they pass on to someone else. The boy is withdrawn, and even in relations with his family there's something off, which he adds of his own accord.

It will all end well. Hatred, suspicion, jealousy are regional products. Unwilling to waste time on love, people polish up the other passions. It's not that these folks are worse than others; it's that, individualists to an extreme and incurably solitary, they're constantly afraid of being duped. And if love does that often (makes you a dupe), hatred never does; there you're on solid ground. I love you: that's never sure; proof is needed. I hate you: that's solid as gold bullion. It shouldn't be concluded that this is some kind of Wild West – that's a misunderstanding perhaps created in part by the fact that firearms are widely used, and from the description of the landscape. Long before the Americans discovered that the West was far away, this land here was already acting like ancient China. Here hatred does not kill: it plays billiards; people who hate one another appear to be fond of each other; which in fact is the case. They're often seen together; you might almost say, always. On many occasions they bill and coo; they go so far as to help one another out. It's the opposite of the Montagues and the Capulets. They could meet in the middle of the desert, nothing would happen, or if it did it would be something nice. They bend over backward for each other, even at their own expense. Naturally there are marriages between families that hate one another – many, in fact. If there weren't any marriages, people would sometimes be in a tight spot. There's marriage, there's keeping company, there's often partnership, there's cohabitation, and it's purest hatred, without the least flaw, tempered in spring water, honed and razor-sharp. What of it, you ask? This: blows originate from very far away, take a very long time to land, and do so via numerous intervening persons. When the blow falls, you'd swear that God alone touched the ax. You need to be far from foolish to be entertained by this little game. All the more because your buddy follows the same paths in the opposite direction, and storing up every drop of rancor against you. This is a highly civilized place. Not the kind where you can strap a pistol to your thigh and make a living by being a faster shot than your adversaries. No, people rather look sleepy, they think for a long time before they speak, but the word they finally utter puts a whole family, sometimes a whole generation, in the crosshairs.

They've traveled dozens, even hundreds of miles to say this word; they've been to agencies, to the offices of swindlers, of men of the law, members of regional parliaments, national politicians, senators, tax assessors and tax collectors, anyone with an ounce of power, anyone who makes birdlime, fox gins, wire-mesh snares, traps, anyone who possesses an office, ink, a penholder, letterhead, summonses with costs and without, anyone who compels you to journeys, expenses, trips down interminable corridors, sleeplessness, anxieties. People make use of their elder daughter, their younger daughter, their wife, their party, their religion (or more precisely, their Church). Since the time this game was first played, any political, financial, administrative, judiciary, notarial, penitentiary, and alcoholic establishment in this *département* and the neighboring ones is at the ready; it bursts into action, snapping its fangs for a single word, a conjunction, the least comma, sometimes a silence. It gobbles up fields, jas, smallholdings, flocks, farmyards, closets, chests, and even people (when the blow works the way it should).

The journeys needed to set this machinery in motion are made in the summer. Or in the heart of an artificial night. The important thing is to conceal the facts and acts of hatred in progress. Everyone is on the alert; the roads are open; where's Ferdinand going, if he's seen getting on the bus? If one of the branches of the Dupuis family is nicknamed Automobile, it's because in 1907 Dupuis the father ruined his daughter-in-law (the wife of his eldest son) by having himself transported in the car of Monsieur Auriol Joséphin, the lumber merchant of Montbrun. It was one of the first cars people had seen, and it was the first time one of those modern devices had been used in the region for such civilizing ends. More recently, if the last of the Cicérons (his two brothers died, one peacefully, the other from an Aleppo boil on his nose) is known as Clarinet Cicéron, it's because he fooled everyone around him by leaving his radio on while he went to Forcalquier to blow the whistle on the trafficking being conducted by Bonardi the Piedmontese (called Biribi, no one knows why). Trafficking in so-called liquor, adulterated of course, but with liquor trafficking it's always plain sailing. There are searches, they turn the place upside down, the house is ransacked along with the stables, the cowsheds, the jas, the barns; when they're done, a mother sow can't even find her little ones. If they don't find anything, that's perfect, because now the idea's been planted in their head, they think they've had the wool pulled over their eyes, and they'll come back and start all over again. It's one of the most spectacular downfalls possible, a delight to watch, and it takes place in installments. Bonardi, of course, fought back – it's not for nothing that he's of Italian origin – but that's not the point.

We spoke a little too briefly of love. As concerns the practices of young folks, there's no need to go back over what's already been said. It might be possible to find the occasional couple gazing at each other inanely, little fingers hooked together; but inanity is not to be believed, it's a sham, it's only there out of tradition. Those are simply calm people who aren't rushing things, but at the end of their little track there's a crash, as with everyone else. On the other hand, the region has many a Philemon and Baucis. Their story lies a little outside the description of the summer. It's purest love, which cannot be expressed in a single season. So it was, for instance, with Long Titus and Camille.

Twenty years ago, I often used to cross that territory every which way. It reminded me of the Scottish moors, which I still missed. I would stay at a solitary inn that was miles from any inhabited place. It was a simple little jas at the crossroads of trails where a passing wanderer could find a glass of beer or wine. For me there was also some pretty agreeable grub, which ranged from thrush and plover to sausage with cabbage, and there was a straw mattress in a lean-to. Camille, who kept the inn, was an old friend. At that time she was seventy-two, but she was fresh as a laurel leaf. In her youth she'd been the prettiest, the most beautiful girl in the whole area. Nothing was left of that but her extraordinary jet-black hair without a single white strand. She hadn't married; she lived alone.

I would arrive at her place without advance warning. Five times out of ten I'd find the doors open, while no one responded to my call. I recognized the signs. I'd go down to the cowshed and find my Camille there, dead drunk, unconscious, lying beneath the cows' feet in the dung and urine. She was a sizable woman. I limited myself to pulling her by the arm or leg away from the animals (and in fact that was all that could be done). For the rest, I had a drill: I'd go up to her bedroom and, if it was daytime, I'd hang a white rag on the latch of the shutter; if it was dusk or nighttime, I'd light a candle or a kerosene lamp, which I'd place in the window. There was nothing left to do but wait.

The wait was at least an hour, in bad weather much longer. The person I was waiting for was coming from far away, and he was no longer a young man: Titus, known as Long, was seventy-eight at the time. He would respond to the summons in any conditions. One time it was in a raging gale. The phrase is no exaggeration: he covered the last hundred yards on all fours after having been blown over a dozen times along the way. He would arrive, see me, and understand at once. Together, the two of us were able to lift Camille and carry her up to her room. He would always take the head, and I'd take the legs. We'd lie the drunken woman on the floor and go down to the kitchen to heat some water; when it was ready I'd help Titus carry up the kettle, the bathtub, and the soap. After that I'd leave him alone; it was his business. He'd only call me back once Camille had been washed from head to foot and he'd given her some clean underwear. We'd combine forces again (it really did require it) to put the ample old lady in her bed. She was so drunk she didn't even wake up during all these operations. At most she'd mumble something or other. He'd tuck her in, and we'd go back down to the kitchen.

We had extensive conversations, Titus and I. He'd been nicknamed Long not for his height – he wasn't tall but rather stocky, with his neck stuck in his shoulders – but because he took an infinite length of time to do things. What an unskillful man would finish in two hours, Titus, who was very skillful (in everything), would take two days to do. So it was with any task. He was the son of Armless Titus. Armless Titus had two arms. He'd acquired his nickname because he always wore his jacket over his shoulders without putting his arms in the sleeves, which dangled empty on either side; hence Armless – that was all it took. Armless had married a sack of gold: Léa, the only daughter of the Romualds, who were known for being simultaneously wild folks and the owners of the fine farm of Roquette. With Léa, Armless had two children: a daughter by the name of Adonise, and then our famous Long Titus. When Armless died, Adonise had already been married to Paul-Émile, the grocer of Banon, for five years. There was an arrangement between brother and sister concerning Roquette, which Titus ran on his own. He hadn't married. Léa died a short time later.

Roquette is an important farm: a jas for a hundred sheep, sizable stables with mangers for more than six horses, barns to match, living quarters with at least a couple dozen large or small rooms, and acreage that didn't amount to very much, being wilderness pure and simple, but woods that could be turned to good account if need be. Long took up quarters in a first-floor room, he reduced the operations of the farm to what he could manage without the help of anyone else, and in the end he made do with the resources provided by the raising of fifty sheep. It has to be said that within a few years he'd become a past master at living within the bounds of a closed economy.

It was the time when, three miles away, Camille was like a

springtime at its height. She too was unmarried – well, not married in front of the mayor. Camille had had an unusual life. She preferred her liberty to family life. In a place where the most manly men encircle themselves with fortifications of every kind of wood, it was a decision more heroic than that of El Cid Campeador. Her character shone in the blue (it cannot be called anything but adamantine) of her eyes, and in her raven-black hair, which she kept into extreme old age. Beautiful and shapely – shapely according to peasant norms, which call for a dependable solidity – on top of it all she was pretty, which is to say, on a human scale. She had many admirers. She didn't make those she chose languish. Her tastes could be extravagant; at one point there was a scandal which I cannot speak of, but which made waves all the way to the bishop's palace. Carried away in describing her beauty and its consequences, I've forgotten to mention that Camille, who was orphaned early in life, had been raised by an uncle who in all probability had taken her innocence when the time came, and eventually left her a sizable inheritance. She didn't need to worry about the future – on condition, of course, that she led the kind of life people lead here. That didn't worry her; she knew how to live modestly except where her free-dom was concerned. She could survive for months on bread, salt, and olive oil, so long as she could give herself the kind of good times she liked.

From the beginning of my conversations with Long Titus, he made no secret of the fact that he'd loved Camille for more than sixty years. He also told me right away that he'd "never asked for anything and never gotten anything." It wasn't out of bashfulness. When men fought over Camille, he joined in; but once he was victorious (which happened three times), he would go back to Roquette. He would let the defeated man enjoy himself, if he was still capable. Because those were true battles between men. One Easter Monday, four of them ganged up on him and broke his arm; another evening he was ambushed a hundred yards from his place by woodsmen who left him for dead, spread-eagled in his own farmyard. But he also remembered heads he'd cracked, notably at the time of the scandal. He confessed to me that at that period he'd gladly have killed. The man Camille was favoring was made of different stuff and didn't take part in the combats. Those men fought for Camille the way people fight for the Tsar. Then the guy made of different stuff was assigned to another parish, and the old vigil of Camille's admirers continued as before.

Pride there was, plainly, in Long Titus. At Saumane he met

a cousin of his who'd served as a colonial sergeant. This fellow taught him some tricks, in particular how to use his feet: a sort of savate, half bayonet fighting, half boxing, half whatever you like, but it worked a charm. The feet came into play at very precise moments and smashed exactly what needed to be smashed. It was unbeatable. People began to be afraid of him. He wasn't keeping them away from Camille, because the moment his back was turned they hopped into bed with her, and he knew it. He fought for the sake of fighting: pride.

It's clear that at the time of all these battles, Titus had elevated the love he felt for Camille on a towering pedestal. Perhaps he was lying to himself, but he remained true to his lie. When his nether parts bothered him a little too much, he would pay a visit to the widow with the tricolor flag. His sister tried to find a wife for him. He resisted, she insisted; she came and played mother hen at Roquette. A house as big as that was made for a family. She had girls lined up; some of them weren't bad, promising well for the future. Titus began at once to reduce the number of farm buildings to his own scale. He took off four fifths of the roof, leaving it only over the room where he lived. Bad weather took up the job, and in a few months had reduced the rest of the place to ruins. Elder bushes and nettles invaded the room where

Armless Titus had died and the one where Long Titus had been born. That shows how proud he was.

Was he jealous? When I put the question to him, he chewed on his mustache for a long while. Yes. And one day, he'd decided to go to Marseille. Which was tantamount to saying, to the Antipodes! An hour on foot, then three hours by bus, then four hours by train. Why Marseille? Because he wanted to buy a long-distance glass. Not binoculars: a telescope like the one held by Admiral Villeneuve at the Battle of Trafalgar. (He had an engraving at home.) One day he showed me what, using the old expression, he called his "spyglass." It was a splendid instrument, still in mint condition since he'd taken such good care of it. It had cost an arm and a leg. When collapsed, it fitted in a round leather case that could be carried over the shoulder.

To begin with, from Roquette he couldn't see Camille's house; he had to climb a beech so as to get above the other trees. He'd have needed to spend all his days up there. He decided to make an opening in the woods. The trees were white oak. He spent months at the task. He cut a three-yard-wide swath directly toward the goal, the way these days they make room for a power line through a forest. Now he no longer needed to climb the beech tree. He could keep an eye on Camille while sitting outside his house, in summertime, and from his fireside in the winter. Keep an eye on her "disinterestedly," what's more, since the time of the battles had passed; people went to Camille's in all innocence. Titus restricted himself to counting the visitors with the aid of his telescope – which, he told me, did not cause him undue suffering. I strove to understand his indifference. It can be explained. In our conversations around the stove, while Camille was sleeping off the wine in her white sheets, Titus often repeated to me: "No one could take her from me. As you see! I'm the one who has her, and I'm keeping her."

He doesn't see her the way she is. He sees her the way he wants her to be. Neither the beautiful ravenhead nor the poor drunk. Her beauty had been impossible to control, even with gunshots – except if she'd been the one he shot at. Titus isn't the type who kills what he loves (as it's generally recognized everyone does to one degree or another). This region is so poor that no one destroys anything, neither what they love nor what they loathe; they keep everything, the good and the bad, because they know that whatever it is, one fine day they might have need of it. He made do. With Camille, he gave himself joys and woes: woes for having joys, joys for having woes; and he did it so well that he spent his entire life at it. He only sees the poor drunken woman as she is, sprawling in manure, at the moment when he knows he's going, with hot water, clean sheets, fresh underclothing, and love, to make her the way he wants her to be. And no one can take her away from him any longer. Has anyone in fact ever done so?

The bridle path, the avenue he cut through the woods for the spyglass over forty years ago, has always been carefully maintained; nothing blocks the line of sight between Roquette and Camille's house. At Roquette, the telescope rests on a little permanent stand on the windowsill. Its purpose is no longer to count admirers but to watch for the appearance of the white rag on the latch of the shutter or the light shining in the window. I still talk of it in the present, yet it's almost three years since Adonise and Paul-Émile's grandson came and took away the spyglass. Titus died during the warm season, fortunately, because that meant he was found at once by the shepherd from Villard. Camille died the next day. I was naive enough to ask about the cause: they replied (since they're not naive) that she died of death. Which, upon reflection, was enough for me. The telescope path has filled in with new trees.

Here we are far from the summer. It remains to describe its

nights – above all the nights when there's no moon. Nothing could be darker; nothing could glimmer more. There are so many stars, they're so clear, so clean, so well buffed by the wind, that they provide a kind of light. In reality it's not light (actually it's the opposite): it's a golden powder with which they cover all objects and all shapes. The light of the sun, or of the moon, which is its reflection, makes shadows. The phosphor of the stars does not make shadow; it reveals the face of the world by sprinkling it, not by illuminating it; it doesn't originate from a precise spot, like a ray of sunshine or the glow of the moon, it comes at the same time from every point in the sky and it makes the inside and the outside of objects gleam at the same time and with the same brightness. It has no orient, it falls like rain from everywhere at once.

Such nights do not calm, they disconcert. They speak not of the periodic vanishing of the sun, but of its permanent disappearance. It's the world without sunlight, but nothing says it will return; rather, everything says it will not. You don't need to be a scholar to understand this; such a night can only go on forever. And even when you know the sun will come back, the most natural, most ancient part of the soul amuses itself by imagining that it no longer does. It's a game at which simple beings are past masters. They replace the anxieties of civilization with the anxieties of the primitive world.

In the villages and at the farms, certain of which are as large as villages, on summer evenings people occasionally bring their chairs out and put them on the doorstep. They get some fresh air. The air always has an exquisite quality like that of spring water. But once the night posts its great constellations up above the street or over the farmyard, the people go back in and bar the door. Shotguns are of no use, only sleep; or a particular kind of passion. And it's here that we rejoin Ennemonde.

If anyone should find this surprising, let's not forget that the High Country is far from large. From west to east, which is to say from the valley separating the Ventoux from Lure all the way to Sisteron, it's about thirty-five miles, and from north to south, in other words from the valley of the Jabron to Route Nationale 100, it's maybe ten or fifteen more. There are only two small towns, two villages, six hamlets of less than twenty residents, and about fifty farms: all these inhabited places, incidentally, being located at the edges of wilderness. In such a small area and with so few people, you can't help meeting the same ones repeatedly. All the more because these people are larger than life.

Honoré was still alive, but "shrunken" in the extreme and reduced to the smallest share in his own house. Ennemonde had taken charge of the shotgun and of her two eldest sons. She was no longer the guileless candidate for anything "normal" (even school). Nor, above all, was she any longer the little girl in love in the ubacs near the Croix Pass. Fifteen years in a nightshirt with a hole in it will sort a woman out properly as far as her mind is concerned. As for her body, thanks to multiple pregnancies it had come to resemble the bodies of all the women of the High Country: it bore only the most distant relation to the human form. Her face was agreeable, despite the loss of all her teeth; her lips were full enough to remain in bloom. She had an attractive fresh, pink complexion; her brown eyes were extremely pure, without wrinkles or dark shadows, and were lined with long curving lashes. Their gaze was sometimes that of a young girl, most of the time not. She weighed over two hundred eighty pounds, but she moved with amazing agility. Men joked about the size of her thighs, without ever having seen them, of course. Despite her weight and her large limbs, she was easily capable of covering twelve miles on foot in five hours, on difficult paths. She had milk-white skin, having always protected it from the sun under a hat, long sleeves, and high collars, like all men and women who know what the sun really is. She wasn't a woman who could be quickly explained. Those who saw her daily, daily wished to uncover her mystery: there was all this monstrousness, that they imagined to be milky and soft, moving under her skirts, and the look in those lovely eyes. That gaze led them to be cautious: not because it was hostile, but quite the opposite.

In 1930 she bought a used Citroën B14 so she could go to the cattle markets. Samuel, her eldest, was her driver. The roads were poor. At the Croix Pass, where she'd had her love story with Honoré, the surface had been worn away by the sheep's feet. When you were traveling at night or in cloud, you had to hammer on the lanterns with your fist to have a bit of light. In good weather, the descent from the pass was truly invigorating. Samuel kept his calm; he was young, he'd seen his mother's coup d'état succeed, nothing surprised him any more; he drove down at top speed. Ennemonde relished it.

The Croix Pass, whose full name is Croix de l'Homme Mort or Dead Man's Cross, links the plateau to the lowlands of the north. If you look closely, on that side there are gorges. They're barely noticeable when you travel by foot, because you don't look down on the flatlands from plunging cliffs, and the eye has time to rest on steep yet wooded slopes. The walker usually says that from the road the view is splendid. In reality, toward Montbrun there's a drop in elevation of over two thousand feet in three miles as the crow flies, while toward Les Freissinières, the descent is two and a half thousand feet. The route is cut into crumbly schist. Even today, despite being paved, supported with walls, and bordered by parapets, the road keeps Bridges and Highways plenty busy. It deteriorates very quickly, gnawed at by frosts and thaws, and by the oozings and runoffs of spring. The people of the High Country rarely take it; they prefer the roundabout route via Sault and Montbrun, adding thirty miles to their journey. Three decades ago, the way was maintained by the road mender. Which is to say, in the course of the summer he would walk it with a shovel over his shoulder.

If someone had told Ennemonde to take the long route through Sault, Montbrun, Barret, and so on, since the Croix Pass road was closed because of bad weather, she'd have replied that she didn't have a minute to lose. It was true. She was forty-one years old. She threw herself into the little northern valleys the way people throw themselves into sin; like sin, those valleys were shadowy, fragrant, and covered with scrub. At the base of the slope, the road entered winding corridors. It wove back and forth across streams that in summer contained nothing but rocks, but which could suddenly swell to a flood twelve or fifteen feet high after a storm. It trampled aromatic carpets of thyme, savory, and lavender; it pushed against thickets of alder and willow smoking with pollen. It passed through shaded spots of unutterable sweetness. Samuel, who would turn off the engine at the pass and coast down the entire slope, his big shoes hitting the foot brake with all his strength at the curves, was always astounded at the prodigious speed he built up during the descent: he would not need to turn the engine back on till they reached the first poplars of Les Freissinières. As for Ennemonde, she let herself be swept along. It was magical. Weight and volume lost all significance: she was a feather flying in the wind. The bumps sent her, not down into the abyss, but up toward the heavens. For the first time she was dealing with strong liquor. Depending on whether a bend pushed her to the left or to the right, she would lean up against the horizon over Montbrun, to the point of touching the setting sun, or against the great glaciers of the Alps, beyond which night was rising. If the journey was being made in the morning, on one side she would rub her cheek on the winds of the dawn, and on the other rise like a swallow above the mists containing Montbrun. From time to time she'd look over at her handsome Samuel, who was driving, equally detached from earthly happenings, barely holding the steering wheel with two fingers. If Honoré had been able to see them, if above all he'd still been capable of taking an interest in them, he'd have said the two of them were rooted in sin, comfortable in sin, come to port in sin.

She managed everything perfectly, did Ennemonde. Her market dealings were negotiated down to the last centime. She almost always got the highest price. The brokers weren't used to dealing with a woman; with widows sometimes, but widows aren't women. She was perfect at running the business of the home, and her personal business too – the latter without fully realizing it. She didn't even know that she'd had (for twenty years) a personal matter to settle, and that she was engaged in doing so.

After the hamlet of Les Freissinières, the road entered a rift between two red rock faces. The passage of the B14 summoned clouds of crows out of the depths. Exiting the defile, you came out above an expanse of open ground carpeted with foxtail grass, dotted with Italian poplars and little gardens, in the middle of which a sort of fortified town curled up like a snail shell, crested with an ironclad bell tower and surrounded with boulevards where the market was held.

It was a small settlement that for a very long time had remained Huguenot and that little by little had become worse.

It was places like this that produced the nightshirt with the hole. There was no need to go ferreting about in the local hosieries: you only needed to look at the shops and the "proprietors." Everything here was cramped and dirty; the people had mouths that chewed on coal. The darkness of the gorges in their tangle of valleys blew through the streets without managing to cleanse them of a stench of Bible. The Protestants of these parts had since time immemorial protested against Protestantism. They'd ended up worshipping anything at all, so long as the anything at all demanded intolerance. Crowns of thorns were consumed in every household, at every meal. Religion was a sort of commerce in which discomfort was always preferred to joy, scorn to pleasure, and ultimately vice to virtue.

The market took place on the boulevards – the right term here, for they truly were raised flat areas running below the old ramparts. They were planted irregularly with wild acacias, Italian poplars, mulberry trees, elderberry bushes, blackberries and hawthorn. Temporary pens contained small flocks that people had brought to sell. Ennemonde had no need to show her animals. She was known, they called her Big Woman, they knew she sold sheep of top quality. She would roam the market ground with her Samuel at her side, and it wouldn't be long before she was approached by brokers. She had her price, decided upon in advance, and she wouldn't budge. In the early days they tried to talk to her about the customary price of meat and other twaddle, but she didn't give a hoot, and so sales were settled quickly: either they accepted her price or they didn't, there was no middle ground; and if they didn't, someone else soon would.

It was a tradition that she treated herself to dinner – with Samuel, of course. Samuel was her guardian angel. Her eyes were damp as she looked at him. She never let go of his arm, holding him tight against herself. After the gorges of the journey, all these men had a dizzying smell of billy goat. She felt in danger. It's those that have the greatest talent for hell who grumble the most before the flames.

In 1932 and 1933, in those parts, people still lived the way they did at the turn of the century. The Hôtel des Tilleuls where Ennemonde dined had kept its traditions: people would all eat together at the *table d'hôte*, with a single dish on the menu from January 1st to New Year's Eve: braised beef stew. It was cooked nonstop for 365 days and 365 nights in a massive cauldron hanging in the hearth of the dining room. The fire was only put out on the night of December 31st to January 1st; at that time the cauldron was emptied, cleaned, and the stew for the approaching year was begun; the fire was relit and come what may. The stew was enhanced in hunting season with hare and boar, sometimes even fox, though in moderation, just for the aroma.

The table d'hôte was the real thing: the landlord himself presided, welcomed his customers, and ate with them. On regular days he even saw to the conversation. On market days, of course, that was out of the question, as was the normal custom of reserving places for women to the host's right. The service was similarly simplified. As the diners entered they passed a dresser where they took a porringer, which is to say a large soup bowl, and also a glass, a fork, and a knife, and they took their seats at the table, arranging their place settings in front of them. Right away each person was served a two-pound loaf of bread and a quart of wine, and their bowl was filled at the cauldron. Diners had the right to a complimentary second bowl of stew, but they had to pay extra if they ordered more bread and wine, which often happened.

It regularly happened to Samuel, who would eat more than two pounds of bread at this meal; Ennemonde took her second helping of stew, drank her quart of wine, but didn't finish all her bread. More than anything she liked the heavy bronzed sauce of melted lard and virgin oil. Each time she would make sure to bring a soup spoon from home tucked away in her blouse, and at table she'd take it out so she could drink the sauce like broth. Her iron-hard gums chewed the long-cooked meat without difficulty. All in all it was a feast. Doubly so: her belly full, she would venture to move away from Samuel, mentally speaking, and even lose sight of him. She would give herself up to a giddiness akin to what she experienced on the road. She saw herself about to scandalize this hypocritical little town. She was no longer rubbing against skies and great heights, sunsets and dawns, but against men who smelled of goat.

One day, as she left the hotel she noticed a crowd gathered in front of the Soubeyran Gate, where the horse market was held. She went up. A wrestler in a tight-fitting pink singlet was standing on a mat. He was calling for challengers, specifying that this was Greco-Roman wrestling. He pointed to a red velvet cushion to which medals were pinned. One of them, he said, was the White Elephant, which had been awarded to him by the King of Siam for defeating a famous Chinese wrestler.

The finger indicating the cushion with the medals caught Ennemonde's attention: it was huge. As she brought her gaze from the finger to the arm, and from the arm to the rest of the body, she was dazzled by a beauty of a kind much to her liking. There was a mass of fat and muscle five feet three tall and five feet wide; he had no neck. The head was planted directly onto the shoulders, attached by a nape that bulged like an August melon. He had neither gaze, nor nose, nor mouth worthy of the name. You could see him breathing the way a rock or a block of iron might breathe, and it was just as startling. Ennemonde began breathing to his rhythm. She was bewitched by the man's hair: half-bald, he wore it brilliantined, meticulously parted on the side, with a kiss curl on the forehead.

She dreamed of it all that night. She felt herself being swept away. How good it was!

She had to wait a month to find another market. The time dragged. She kept thinking of the Greco-Roman braced against a blacksmith who'd picked up the gauntlet. There was much more of a future in those muscles than in any number of head-spinning roads. She walked all around the market in vain; she saw no gathering and no wrestler. She looked and looked till nighttime, and then she had to leave.

The blacksmith who'd fought with the wrestler had a small mechanic's shop on the boulevard, where he sold farm machinery. After passing twenty times in front of the forge, where the smith was working the bellows, she took the plunge, went in, and made inquiries. The owner of the White Elephant was known to everyone as Clef-des-Coeurs, Key-of-Hearts; the blacksmith couldn't tell her his real name. He only came here when there wasn't a more important market elsewhere. Today there was a good chance he'd be at Carpentras, where there was a sausage market, the biggest one of the year. Ennemonde's first instinct was to head to Carpentras, even though night had fallen. But there was Samuel. They had to go home.

Once there, she immediately checked the post office calendar, before she even greeted her family. The next big market was at Orange in forty days. That was far. Never mind the forty days, she had come to terms with that; but Orange . . . She'd never been there. She had no excuse for going. She didn't know the dealers there, they didn't know her. And there was always Samuel. Some maneuvering was needed.

She did some. First, she learned to drive the B14. She succeeded at once: she had the Greco-Roman before her eyes. Then she took Samuel aside and talked to him about family. Her children adored her. She lectured her eldest, who listened dutifully. They could no longer count on their father. A man was needed as head of the household. Samuel was cut out for the job. His brothers obeyed him; for his sisters his every word was law. Their father was no longer much of anything, but it's precisely when someone is no longer much of anything that they want to become something else. It could easily happen that, one day when she and Samuel were in town, his father would grab the shotgun and try to put things back the way they used to be. She'd been thinking about it a lot; that was why she'd been distracted of late. She wrapped it all up in a lot of sweet words. Samuel didn't need that. He took his role seriously.

She took flight on November 16th. She said she was going to Orange. She was planning to come back that night, but they shouldn't worry if it was the next day. She encountered some iced-over snow at the entrance to the gorges of the Nesque. Since she knew next to nothing about driving a car, in the state she was in she enjoyed the skidding greatly: it was a dance. She came back that evening. She'd seen Clef-des-Coeurs. And above all, he had seen her. Peasant women are not in the habit of watching wrestling contests, even Greco-Roman ones; rather, they make a show of keeping their distance. Whereas Ennemonde was in the front row, eyes shining, lips gleaming, cheeks aflame. And then there was her size!

She'd even conducted some business. She wanted to have a justification for everything.

It was at Séderon in the spring that Clef-des-Coeurs finally spoke to her. He did more: he invited her for a glass of champoreau, which she drank. They were sitting side by side on the bench. He placed his hand on Ennemonde's thigh. There was plenty of room for it. He told her the story of his life: the King of Siam, the White Elephant, the gold medal from the market at Avignon, the time in Tarascon when in one minute he brought down the Bull of Vaucluse; how he was shy, he was alone; he kneaded the thigh. He smelled of violets; it was the brilliantine. He led Ennemonde into the fields, and she got exactly what she'd been waiting for.

Clef-des-Coeurs was dazzled; this was the first heart he had opened. The tenderness knocked him sideways. Curiously or otherwise, his name was Joseph Quadragésime. He was a foundling, which is no laughing matter; he was found at Uzès, which is worse; and in 1898, which is the worst of all. It was a time and a place where people did not pussyfoot around with love. He had nothing in the way of a childhood, or at least nothing that was childlike, rather the opposite. Until the day when he was big enough to defend himself. After he flattened his last boss (a steward at the poorhouse), he had five or six days of complete youthful freedom in the scrublands north of Nîmes, followed by a year of prison. When he got out he signed up for seven years in the Foreign Legion. At Sidi Bel Abbès he had a heart tattooed on his chest, on the right-hand side of course. The tattooist was an old Englishman who was fond of symbols. After his time was up, Quadragésime did not re-enlist. He was wrestling champion for the entire military region. It was a job. At Marseille he entered Paul Pons's gym, *Au Paradis des Athlètes*. After that, there was nothing, until Ennemonde. He truly was shy and alone.

Ennemonde made her mind up at once. The happiness she'd just experienced was long overdue, and she had every right to it. It was out of the question to continue going to all the markets and sleeping together in the bushes. While Clef-des-Coeurs, who was sentimental, walked her back holding her by the little finger, she was thinking at high speed. In this way, she suddenly remembered the house of Jules Dupuis, known as Wagtail (whose head had still not been found). This house, hidden in the very darkest of the ubacs of Pompe, was exactly what was needed as they waited. Waited for what? For what was in the back of Ennemonde's mind. The Melchior Dupuis had abandoned this out-of-the-way place, which had furthermore been battered every day by the winds, the rains, and the permanent shade of the ubacs. Only a man like Wagtail could have lived there, and only a man like the one presently holding her by the little finger could live there now, while they waited. He would be within reach for her; it was a matter of an hour's journey to join him each night. The Greco-Roman agreed to everything. Given the state of his right-hand heart and his left-hand heart, he couldn't refuse anything of this woman whose voice was like the cooing of a woodpigeon. The suitcase containing the rug, the White Elephant, and the singlet was loaded into the B14.

Above the pass Ennemonde concealed the car beneath an oak and, taking a shortcut, led Clef-des-Coeurs to the house. It was the first of many nights. There was the great covering of the stars, but at ground level there were animal ghosts. Had the regional army champion lacked passion, it would have been too much for him, especially on the ubacs; but three hundred pounds of love has a funny effect on someone who weighs two forty and up till now has only ever tasted featherweights.

The house on the ubac wasn't exactly a palace. The first evening they even had to drive a badger out of it. But bit by bit, thanks to the resourcefulness of the Greco-Roman and all the materials brought by Ennemonde – sheets, cooking utensils, stove, even a table and chairs – it was licked into shape. The place was entirely satisfactory. All the more, as the lover herself said, because it was only a temporary arrangement. She saw the future. She even saw how to craft it. Clef-des-Coeurs had made a huge bed with a litter of beech leaves. That was the most important thing.

Getting through the summer was hard. The nights were too short; Ennemonde could only leave her house very late, and she had to be back before daybreak. But she did it, regularly, without missing a day. By mid-autumn their patience had paid off; now the season was on their side. Every night Ennemonde had to battle rain and wind; soon she'd have to reckon with cold, snow, and the fierce north wind that blows from the Alps and whose howling is so romantic; but all she saw were the nights getting longer.

They found in this arrangement the certainty that they understood one another perfectly. Above all Ennemonde: she needed it, having so much still to do to reach her goal. She often studied her face in the mirror. She found it beautiful, and rightly so: it *was* beautiful. The eyes had no equal for many miles around, even among the young women; the rest of the face was full and luminous. The complete absence of teeth was not a hindrance; on the contrary, her rather full lips took on a more malicious shape; the malice rendered more human and less divine the flawless purity of her gaze, which otherwise might have seemed a little vacant. Her body? Dear Lord, the body was spoiled only in the chest. Her bust, of course, sizable yet soft, and which had nourished thirteen children, was not accessible to just anyone; but Clef-des-Coeurs was not just anyone. She knew what his hands were seeking and finding when they caressed her body. Clef-des-Coeurs was moved less by the form of this flesh than by its purpose. And as for that purpose, the rest of the body catered to it perfectly.

Often during that long winter, in the great bed of beech leaves which filled the room, between the white sheets that Ennemonde had selected from her bridal trousseau as being the most lovely (Honoré had never wanted to use them), under thick blankets and sheepskins, they would linger, clasped together yet motionless.

It was during one of these moments that they heard someone trying the door. No, it wasn't Honoré; Honoré, as she was well aware, would have gone about things in a biblical manner; she knew that and was counting on it. Nor was it the Melchiors; the Melchiors, certain of their rights, would have rattled the door. This was someone poking about – someone unaware that the Melchiors knew their business when it came to locks and bolts. It was the dead of winter; the person did not persist, and they heard whoever it was walk away, the snow crunching underfoot.

It had to have been someone with Wagtail's million on their mind. Ennemonde told Clef-des-Coeurs the story.

People are happy or they're unhappy, but the earth turns; after the spring they could feel summer approaching. Now, Ennemonde had never lost sight of the earth. This spring was its boundary. One evening, as she left the house, she deliberately made a noise as she passed the bakehouse where Honoré slept, barricaded in. The next day she repeated her ploy. The door remained barred. It took eight days. She was not surprised; she'd anticipated this. You don't have thirteen children with a man through a nightshirt with a hole in it without learning how he's going to react. She could almost have warned Clef-des-Coeurs; she didn't, because the stakes were too high – her entire future. It was the right decision. On the ninth day, coming back home she found Honoré standing in the yard. Finally he was up and about; he wanted to know where she'd been. Two hours later, he was found beneath the hooves of the mule.

Ennemonde was a woman of great sense – wise, clear-headed; she conducted herself in an open, even, consistent way, and on top of it all she was an admirably orderly housewife. Her eight surviving children swore by her and her alone. They were well cared for; the house gleamed; her finances were flourishing. She'd never cheated anyone of the least sou. Her size had long kept her safe from the jealousies of other women (regarding which, as we have seen, they were wrong; in these parts, though, the jealousies of women are not farsighted). There was never even a question of refusing permission to bury him. The house on the ubac was vacated; its tenant had disappeared. All that remained was to make it through the summer. She went twice to Draguignan, once to Séderon. That was all.

In October of the same year, Ennemonde received a visit from a front-wheel drive automobile that contained a personage – a fine-looking man in terms of build, according to the standards of the region, where faces were never part of the equation; he was nicely turned out – modestly, but nicely, because he sported a horseshoe-shaped tiepin. It was Clef-des-Coeurs. He'd grown a mustache and arranged his hair with a part in the middle and no kiss curl, which changed him completely. In addition, he was wearing a fedora.

Ennemonde went into loud delights in front of her family. It was Cousin Joseph! Had those in the High Country forgotten about Cousin Joseph, who'd left for Algeria? Well, it was him. It seemed he'd made his fortune over there. This cousin (a distant relative, she said) had been officially recognized by Martin of

Montbrun, who himself was a first cousin of Ennemonde's. As proof, Martin even mentioned that Joseph had paid back on the nail the money he'd borrowed from the family before emigrating over the seas. It must have been a tidy sum, because at Sisteron Martin put in an order for a brand-new bus, with which he was planning to set up a new route in the Jabron valley. He didn't manage to do it: Martin liked a fight, the money gave him itchy fists, and he was killed before he could even take his new wheels for a spin, by a Piedmontese who was arrested at Laragne and tried at Gap. That, of course, was a matter of chance; but of reasoned chance. You can't always do everything on your own; you have to rely a little (judiciously) on others.

It was hard to send Cousin Joseph away on those terrible winter nights – for he came back to visit frequently. He seemed to enjoy the company of the whole family. They enjoyed his company too. He told stories about the Arabs, and he even knew how to perform card tricks; then he brought a radio set as a gift. All this done with moderation. On the one hand there was Samuel, who was getting ready to leave for the army; his brother David, who was eighteen; and the three girls: Judith, Noémie, and Rachel, seventeen, sixteen, and fifteen respectively. They had been born during Honoré's great biblical period. The next two children had died in infancy. They were spoken of vaguely: Rodolphe and Andréa. Both had seen the light of day at the beginning of Ennemonde's revolt, when she'd been trying to think no more of the nightshirt with the hole, and to escape toward romance. After that came the last three surviving children: Ferdinand, Alithéa, and Chantal, twelve, eleven, and ten, born in the very middle of the escape. Ennemonde's last three pregnancies, impeded precisely by her flight, had not borne fruit that could be remembered, except for the very last, who she had insisted on naming simply Paul, which suggests that at that moment she was already resolved to enter the present century. The most resistant of the children (though within the bounds of reason) were Judith, Noémie, and Rachel. That was to be expected. Ennemonde had been ready for it. Rachel yielded first, after being taken seriously, like a young lady, for a month at a stretch. Judith and Noémie capitulated during a trip by automobile: the way Rachel had been treated had made them highly sensitive to the always violet-scented attentions of Cousin Joseph.

He was a big hit in the village too. It wasn't clear who had alerted him – perhaps he just had a gift – but he was very good at distinguishing between those whose opinion counted and those who could (and even should) be dealt with offhandedly. They accepted him as one of their own.

Clef-des-Coeurs supposedly lived in Orange, or Draguignan, or Avignon, or Marseilles – it was somewhat unclear; but he visited often and stayed for longer and longer in a family that now was thoroughly united, with whom he felt comfortable and who felt comfortable with him. One evening at table Ennemonde announced to him that she was purchasing the whole farm and its pastureland, and as if upon command he began to speak of a dream of his: what if, on one of the old threshing floors, they built a nice, sparkling new house, "with green shutters"? They could each have their own wallpapered bedroom. It could all be centrally heated even; in any case there'd be a bathroom for sure; he reeled off all the pleasures of Babylon, including an "ultramodern kitchen." The children listened openmouthed. Ennemonde replied, timidly (as if enticed but regretful), that she lacked the money for such an undertaking. At that point, on the part of Joseph there were some fine theatricals involving a hand placed on the chest, a "what's mine is yours," a "you're my only family," and an "I love you all as if you were my kin," followed by tears that were most moving in this face whose eyes they had never seen. For the first time, that evening a general hugging and kissing session took place.

Clef-des-Coeurs and Ennemonde had their own hugging and kissing sessions, of course; they'd only refrained during the critical period just after Honoré's death, and while Cousin Joseph was taking his entrance examination before the family and the village. Once extreme caution allowed it, they'd hurriedly resumed quite regular meetings at an "altar of repose" near Apt, more specifically at Goult-Lumières. The bed was small. But it was better than nothing. Eight months of strict fasting had been long, but what had to be had to be, and the goal was close.

A contractor from Banon was given the job of building the new house. He had ideas and an album; he proposed a kind of Swiss chalet. On paper the Swiss chalet looked good, the whole family was thrilled. Samuel had time to see the foundations dug, then he left for his regiment in Valence. Normally the construction of a Swiss chalet at the jas on Pendu Hill would have excited curiosity and jealousy. It so happened, though, that this was 1938 and war was looming. People spoke of the house, but not much; they had other worries.

One day, though, when the truck that brought the workmen each morning arrived, Fouillerot climbed out. He'd told them he had someone to see in the neighborhood, but in fact he lingered all day on the building site, eyeing the dimensions of the new house, computing what it was going to cost. This visit provided a sudden revelation to Ennemonde. She'd kept too close an eye on everything concerning her love to overlook even the slightest detail, above all the time the lock had been fiddled with at the house on the ubac, the night she'd been lying still with her darling. They'd taken precautionary steps the following morning. They hadn't seen anyone, but the fact was there: somebody had tried to enter. Who? She'd gone through everyone. Not Honoré; not this person, not that person; if it had been someone keeping an eye on her, they wouldn't have tried the door. It was somebody looking for the million. She thought about Martin of Montbrun, but these days Martin was pushing up the daisies. Now she got it: it had been Fouillerot. She was more pleased than alarmed.

Fouillerot had two weaknesses: he loved money, and he thought a former bailiff was a somebody. Before he left, he thought it smart to drop a few hints that were perfectly understood. Ennemonde knew that not all game is hunted with the same kind of shot. She had to find the right caliber for Fouillerot. The latter had poked about here, there, and everywhere in the region for over twenty years; no one set aside a sum of any size whatever without consulting him and even following his advice. As well as moneylending, then, he'd "invested shares," and, since he liked a sizable commission, most of these investments carried sizable commissions – so sizable they often ended up no longer sharing anything at all. To be sure, they always looked as if they would; they were convincing enough to be squirreled away in the airing cupboard, like actual shares, but in reality they represented stocks in the Trouser Button Mines or the Timbuktu Streetcar Company. Since in these parts when someone puts something aside it's for good, and things are put aside for at least a hundred years, the bearers of these shares never noticed they were invalid; if by some unlikely chance they needed ready cash, they would go find Fouillerot, who would advise them to sell either French government bonds, or electric company stock, or shares in the Paris-Lyon-Mediterranean Railroad. If they didn't have any government bonds or electric company stock, or railroad shares, which was rare, Fouillerot would advise them to hold onto the Timbuktu Streetcar Company and the Trouser Button Mines, which were "going to go up" and in fact were "on their way up" already, and he would lend them the sum they needed at 7 or 8 percent per month. To pay out the dividends, he convinced people to purchase other shares of the same type, and with the money from those purchases he would pay the dividends from the preceding ones. This ruse went on for more than twenty years.

Ennemonde didn't figure out how this system worked right away, and truth be told, she was far from suspecting the entire mechanism. But in order to determine the appropriate caliber of shot (or buck), she looked into Fouillerot here and there. With her good sense (and her passion) it became clear to her that bit by bit she was bringing to light the springs, pins, and cogs that constituted the essence of Fouillerot. Eventually, she became intrigued by these much-vaunted stocks and shares. She'd studied for teacher training college in her time, after all! That hadn't given her a deep understanding of finance of course, but she said to herself straightforwardly: I know government bonds, I know the electric company, I know the railroad. I know this, I know that, but this other thing I don't know. There was a lot she didn't know, of course, and she didn't unlock the secret right away; as she went to Orange and Carpentras and inquired at the banks, at first she was told: "Yes ma'am, these are good shares, they're well regarded on the stock exchange, they're worth such and such." But one fine day she was told: "No ma'am, that stock doesn't exist. It's worth nothing." Aha, my good fellow!

Obviously, she said to herself, I wish the death of the sinner; she didn't conceive of her decision in exactly those terms, but she needed to ward off permanently any danger that could come from Fouillerot's direction. Because they had in fact found the treasure. Not the million – the million was in numbered Treasury bills that had been officially stopped – but, much better than the million, three thousand gold coins, louis and Swiss currency. Solid proof of heaven's desire to guide the two lovers' happiness with a firm hand. A short time after the night when someone tried the door handle, alerted by the ensuing conversation in which Ennemonde had spoken of the million, Clef-des-Coeurs had undertaken a methodical search of the house and a sounding of the walls; he'd learned a thing or two in the Legion, notably the knitting needle trick. He had the time, and he had the patience. He found the stash and, by the same token, gave Ennemonde an exceptional proof of his love: This man, she said to herself, all her limbs atremble, has never had two pennies to rub together. Here he is with all this gold that he found on his own this afternoon. He could have gone, left me. We've been together three years now; even supposing he loves me, he could prefer gold over me. He waited for me, and he prefers me to all the gold in the world. (She was right: three thousand gold louis and all the gold in the world are the same in this case.) She was enflamed. A splendid night followed, during which Clef-des-Coeurs did not understand a great deal, except the fact that he hadn't ever expected so much, and that Ennemonde was even better than in the early days. As for her, she felt as if she were in a forge. That night had decided everything: the stubborn mule, and that stab of intelligence that had made her bank on the Piedmontese of Sisteron; the eight-month fast; the performance in front of her family – a family she adored – and now, finally, the death of the sinner.

Fouillerot knew of the existence of the three thousand gold coins. He hadn't sold them to Wagtail – not all of them – but he knew that the man with the dogs did business with agencies in neighboring valleys, and there existed a kind of tom-tom network among him and his colleagues. They didn't tell each other everything, but they told each other some things; the rest was a simple matter of interpretation. When he'd gone to the Melchior Dupuis to speak of the Treasury bills and to encourage them to stake claims on them, it was so he could keep an eye on the matter. He had even, a short time later, made a secret proposal, very much in his style. "If by chance you should find the bills," he said to them, "don't tell a soul, come see me. There's no sense in the government sticking its nose into all this, you won't have anything left. Don't worry about the claims, I'll take care of that." He told himself that if need be, he'd work out exactly what the claims amounted to, and give them 10 percent; on top of this possibility, which depended on many things, though you never know, in such a way he also kept in with the Melchiors. So as not to leave anything to chance, he went more than twenty times, by night, to explore the house on the ubac. The twenty-first time, he found the door locked. He wondered for a moment if the Melchiors had taken the initiative, but the Melchiors were primitives; it was impossible to imagine them having the least glimmer of an idea, even the extremely simple one of locking the door. It was someone else, then. He lay in wait. Finally, he heard movements inside, and something like voices. He kept watch till morning. He saw Ennemonde come out. Aha, my lovely friend!

Since Honoré's death, Ennemonde had grown more beautiful. Happiness became her. Her hugeness had settled in itself. Her hair was still black as pitch; her skin light, fine, soft, transparent, with blushings of the liveliest blood. She applied a tiny amount of rouge in the middle of her lips, and powder that smelled of sugared almonds. And her eyes! Such purity! Nothing was as pure as those eyes, their gaze encircled all the way around by lashes three quarters of an inch long. She went alone to see Fouillerot (there was no need to display Clef-des-Coeurs overmuch). The former bailiff, though he'd marinated in official documents for fifty years, was disconcerted by the purity of those eyes; not moved, of course, not affected or softened or anything of that sort, but disconcerted, to the point that he did not understand at first the terms of the letter Ennemonde had just handed him. He was secure in the belief that he had her in the palm of his hand – a conviction reinforced by the fact that she was all dressed up in her Sunday best. What was the meaning of this Crédit Lyonnais letterhead? He raised his eyes; he met a different gaze. Now he set about reading carefully. The matter was simple and clear. It was stated in this letter, which was signed by the manager of a major bank, that the Trouser Button Mines, the Timbuktu Streetcar Company, the Casino of Trifouillis-les-Oies, the Hoggar Wireworks and Rolling Mill, the Rubber Plantations of Cuzco, the Badabada-Oudououdou Railroad, and other alleged Russian bonds were not worth a rabbit's fart and were a matter of pure fraud. All that was needed was to put the word about . . . He tried to fight back. "Their minds will be on what they've lost and the number you've pulled on them," said Ennemonde. "They don't give a good goddam about what I gain and the number I'm pulling on you. Though in fact, try proving that I have anything at all to gain, or that I'm pulling a number. Who'll believe you? Who'll believe a thief?" Fouillerot had a son who was in law school in Aix-en-Provence. A thief? That would be unendurable! Yet here was the letter from the Crédit Lyonnais, and he was better placed than anyone to know that it spoke the truth. He gave in. He thought that was the end of it; he was wrong. Ennemonde did not want to run the slightest risk.

The Swiss chalet was a mistake, she knew it. Her first and only mistake, which would have to be paid for all the same. But God wanted Ennemonde to be happy, and war broke out. They moved into the new house at the moment when Hitler was roaring. Until the defeat of France, Ennemonde thought of Fouillerot. In addition, it was a tough period to get through: the whole family was living together under the same roof, but there was no way of loving freely because of the children. After the fall of the country was announced, things fell into place: Samuel was a prisoner of war; Ennemonde and Clef-des-Coeurs went and married without pomp in Avignon. Anyone would have understood, you needed a man in the house. A marriage of love that would never have been forgiven passed for a marriage of convenience. When the deportations for forced labor began, David joined the resistance. It was easy, all you needed to do was head out. A few fighters of this kind – which is to say, all the young folks in the region of an age to be sent to Germany – took up residence in jas out in the wilderness and on the ubacs. Clef-des-Coeurs supplied them on a regular basis. It wasn't even taking a stand: it was an entirely natural thing. From the moment he saw shotguns and machine guns in their hands, he'd had a come-hither feeling; the Legion was beckoning. In all of this there wasn't a hint of self-interest. It was the slope that God himself places before the feet of His friends. Ennemonde was bringing in the money. She was doing very well on the black market. They'd set up a clandestine butcher's shop in the old house. It wasn't at all disguised; since it supplied not only the resistance in the jas and the ubacs, but that of Séderon and La Bohémienne too, the gendarmes turned a blind eye. It wasn't for lack of anonymous denunciations. In some of them, they thought they discerned the hand of Fouillerot. One morning he was found dead outside his front door. He'd been shot at close range with some very vigorous kind of weapon. He was owed money by all and sundry. His son had the good sense to stay in Aix.

Ennemonde's story was coming to an end; nothing awaited her after the death of Fouillerot, apart from what ordinary people call success. From having stood guard around her happiness, Enne-monde had learned a great deal about the life of the feelings, in particular that pure gold always ends up turning to base lead. She no longer had that ravenous hunger; it was the same for Clef-des-Coeurs, she knew. True, what was left would have gladdened twenty other couples, but after all was said and done, looking at the sacrifices they'd made to raise the four walls of their conjugal bedroom, the question arose whether it had all been worth it. It wasn't a matter of the heart: the heart was on one side, life on the other. She still loved; she was still often transported to heaven. But she also procured a lot of joy, including physical pleasure, in bringing in money. She earned it hand over fist. She kept the whole valley supplied with black-market meat, and she had a sort of tacit authorization, because she provided fully for the insurgents of the ubacs and the mountains all around. The clandestine butcher's shop on Pendu Hill operated day and night; Ennemonde had to travel alone to make cloak-and-dagger deals in Orange, Avignon, Carpentras; she once even went as far as Grenoble and Marseille. She had to knock by night at hidden doors, withstand sinister looks, earn respect. She had to buy people off, "good" people, strong people who grew humble and submissive once she showed them some money. Each time it happened, she felt that stirring sensation, and the delicious hammering of the smithy, that had bound her to Clef-des-Coeurs. It would have been hard for her to give up these new emotions; at times she preferred them to those of the marriage bed. She realized that she had taken deep pleasure in sacrificing Honoré, Martin, even Fouillerot.

"Cousin Joseph" bought the livestock and supervised the slaughtering. Every Wednesday he would take the truck and deliver supplies to the Maquis. It was easy as pie: not only were the Germans far away, they only ever skirted the region. Hide nor hair of any German was ever seen. Clef-des-Coeurs also passed some truly picturesque nights under the stars. He liked being among those young people; he spoke to them of his time in the Foreign Legion. Toward the end of the Occupation, the high wilderness in the mountains was used for arms drops. Clef-des-Coeurs gladly lent a hand in picking up and distributing the manna from heaven. He met delegates from neighboring resistance units with whom he didn't exactly see eye to eye. They demanded the lion's share; he wanted to hold onto a heavy machine gun. (It came from the depository in Orange.) In the end he had his way. He showed David how to look after the gun. He dreamed of it by night. When he was at the Swiss chalet he couldn't sleep thinking of that magnificent weapon. Have they oiled it like I told them to? Are they keeping it in its cover? Whenever he had a free moment he would go there to see it and handle it. One night, lying next to Ennemonde he thought about Abd el-Krim; not for long, just a brief flash, but it was the first time since he'd left the service. And yet before Ennemonde he'd been entirely alone.

Someone spilled the beans about the parachute drops. Seven truckloads of SS with dogs drove up the Banon road to the high wilderness. They hadn't even entered the hairpin bends at Redortiers when Clef-des-Coeurs, alerted by the hubbub, started haring up the short-cuts on the ubacs. Ennemonde was in Avignon that day. He found the camp in turmoil. There were a dozen or more kids of twenty. He showed them how they could be the masters of the ubacs by yielding ground over which the enemy was unable to advance: those north-facing slopes, overlooking the Jabron valley, were extremely steep and covered with large bushes, junipers, white oaks, and interspersed with sheer cliffs. All they had to do was to slip away into this terrain, refrain from trying to cross the valley, and remain in the nearby foothills, from which it would have taken Alexander's army to dislodge them. "I'll make some noise to cover you." And he had them give him the heavy machine gun with five cases of ammunition belts. David insisted on staying with him; Clef-des-Coeurs found that entirely natural, he'd taught him the role of feeder. The two of them had time to dig a foxhole in an excellent location. It overlooked three slopes that rose toward them, the fourth, inaccessible side resting against the cliff to the north.

Air support had to be brought in to silence them. Clef-des-Coeurs had never been at a party like this one. The machine gun rattled away (he'd always wanted a motorcycle!); as he was shooting down SS officers and their dogs he was happy to sense the existence of Ennemonde in the background. He never loved anyone the way he loved David. Toward the evening of the second day, a low-flying plane gunned them down, though it had to make five passes.

Ennemonde wept for months, softly. She was filled with a great sweetness.

She was awoken after the Liberation. She was the wife and mother of heroes. The prefect stood to attention and gave her a military salute. She attended banquets, seated in the place of honor; she presided over others. A representative in the departmental government who was a dentist offered to make her a denture. Free of charge. She accepted. She paid him several visits so he could take casts. He was a ruddy fellow dressed in white – always a delightful combination. But as he leaned over her and her open mouth, she weighed him up and found him too light. No, she said to herself. It's over. And given that it was over, she allowed herself to weigh up everyone around her. Often, at the banquets for liberators that took place almost weekly, she would estimate the weight of certain attendees, letting herself be drawn into dreams by big mustaches, big cheeks, big necks, without feeling the least excitement. No, she would say to herself, it's really over. Besides, she thought constantly of Clef-des-Coeurs, of Cousin Joseph, of Monsieur Quadragésime (whose name she now carried). She'd known him in all his forms, and in all his forms he had fulfilled her. Each time she thought of him, she was surprised at feeling happy that he was dead; then the surprise passed, and she understood that it wasn't happiness but peace, and it wasn't a matter of death but of a separation from the object of her passion. She had come to realize she'd never have had the courage to envisage this necessary separation coolly or to lead it to its logical conclusion, the way she had with Honoré. It was said that she would never handle lead, always gold.

She received her denture in the mail and also, despite the clearly stated intentions of the representative, a bill, which she paid. Samuel, released from prisoner-of-war camp, looked after the flocks and the Pendu jas. Judith and Noémie had married – the first with the elder son from the Café des Boulomanes in Carpentras, a beverage business that was going well. She already had two children. Noémie had wed a tax collector's clerk who'd been part of the Maquis saved by the "sacrifice" of Clef-des-Coeurs and David. This clerk was poised for rapid promotion, but he'd had to accept a position in the Aisne département in the North. The household wrote regularly. Rachel was dating, specifically Siméon Richard of Saumane, the one who'd killed the "horrible thing" and who afterward had been nicknamed Siméon Wolf-Dog. They were both very nice to each other, but neither of them could make up their mind, and since they made no clear move in the summer, people were obliged to await their pleasure. They refused all other matches, they were always together, and no one could see anything about to come of it.

Ferdinand had been spoiled by the Occupation. In 1941 he'd been sent to Avignon High School as a boarder. He could have shone there; instead, he maintained decently average grades. He failed his baccalaureate, refused to retake it, and settled in at the jas, where Samuel greeted him with unparalleled displays of joy. David's death had affected him deeply. Since his return, Ennemonde had urged him to marry; he'd refused, with more energy than was needed in such situations – an energy that looked like anger. He did not seem happy on his own. Ferdinand's arrival transformed him. It was a kind of love. That's fine, Ennemonde said to herself, those boys take after me. She reckoned it would last them a good part of their lives: the time of "base lead" would arrive for them too, but she'd no longer be there, and perhaps the moment itself wouldn't come after all.

The girls took after Honoré. Especially Alithéa: she was a math genius. She was pretty as a picture, but her intelligence had nothing to do with her body, and it was plain as day that she was only interested in intelligence. Her teacher had written to Ennemonde; he was the one who'd spoken of genius. "In all my career," he said, "I've never been confronted with such obvious genius." He offered advice as to which specialization Alithéa should be guided toward, and he spoke of what she'd do after her lower and higher degrees (in the plural), which he considered unimportant formalities. Alithéa was sent to the Polytechnic Institute in Grenoble. As for Chantal, she resolved the question that had been hanging in the air since 1913 and entered the teacher training college at Digne.

The denture made Ennemonde look ugly. She put it in, looked

at herself in the mirror and took it out again: she'd never seen such an ogre-like face! A little later, she noticed her beauty was fading. Despite the excellence of the mirror – it was the one in which, on so many occasions, she had found herself beautiful – she appeared distorted, as if reflected in water. It was old age, into which, little by little, she was sinking. Her size, though it did not increase, became enormity; she felt her weight, she experienced pain and, at the same time, feelings of remorse, which increased as she gradually lost her mobility. Her children had not stopped adoring her; they waited hand and foot on her, especially Samuel and Ferdinand, who took care of the farm, and Rachel, still unmarried, who assumed all the responsibility for looking after the house.

Chantal had obtained a position as schoolteacher in the region. She bought herself a Citroën 2CV and would come visit her mother. Alithéa was in Paris, but she wrote every week with amazing regularity. Her fellow scholars would have been astonished by the tone of her letters. This girl, before whom all the examinations, competitions, and certificates of creation had yielded like snowflakes obliterated on a car windshield, without slowing her advance in the slightest, had only one love: her mother. Love is in fact an inadequate word to describe the feelings she would express in four pages of almost childlike hand-writing every God-given Wednesday: it was the boundless esteem of a student for her beloved master, an inexhaustible babble of admiration. Now, Alithéa was regarded by her peers as being an obvious future Nobel Prize-winner, while Ennemonde had failed her entrance exam to teacher training college. Noémie and her tax collector (who'd been posted to La Manche) also wrote quite regularly. Only Judith, the beverage maker of Carpentras, remained a little distant. This was partly because she'd become very rich, but above all because she'd turned the back room of her café (which had previously contained two billiard tables) into an art gallery. Her two children, who at birth had been named Pierre and Jeanne, she now called Patrick and Ghislaine.

Ennemonde's .pain only made her increase in size and in beauty. Confined to her armchair now, she listened to the past, the way you listen to the sea in a seashell. She surveyed her own actions. Her past amazed her and made her tremble. That's not possible, she would say to herself. You can't have done anything like that, surely? How could you have? It isn't you; it wasn't you; you made it up. Then, once this past appeared in all its details and all it had achieved, she would tell herself: No, it really was you. You did all those things that seem so extraordinary, but in order for them to succeed you had to get your hands dirty, dip them in who knows how many other things that were even more extraordinary and dangerous. She made herself afraid; she shook. She was enraptured. She wept in the most moving fashion, without any comical sounds, like in the great tragedies; big tears filled her eyes and streamed down her cheeks in the manner beloved of the Romantics. Her children would gather around her and console her. At first, these misunderstandings delighted her; in the end she no longer knew if they were misunderstandings at all, and she felt lucky to have such attentive children.

She kept Alithéa's letters in the pouch of her apron. When she'd collected ten of them, she asked for a piece of string to tie them up together, and Rachel would place the bundle in the chest of drawers. It already contained several hundred letters; if a stranger were to have read them one after another, he'd have been struck by the unending litany of adoration that was appallingly monotonous. Whereas at twenty-five Alithéa had published "An Attempt at Perfect Axiomatization in the Study of Invariants and of Lattice Theory," which made her sought after by every scientific institution in the world. She had visited the Soviet Union three times and the United States twice; she'd long been regarded as a scholar with a brilliant future, and she was working on "Doubts Regarding the Identity of Chemical Properties in Isotopic Elements."

One Friday, which was the day the mail was delivered, after reading one of these famous letters that resembled all the others, Ennemonde said: "Tell Alithéa to come." They sent a cable. Alithéa reached Marignane on the Monday, rented a car, and on Tuesday morning she walked into the Swiss chalet. She was as pretty as ever. Winter was approaching, and Ennemonde's armchair had been placed close to the stove. Alithéa kissed her mother and spent a long time stroking the thick white hair that Rachel had fashioned into two coils with a part in the middle. They spoke of this and that. Ennemonde and Alithéa were only alone for a single minute that day, while Rachel went down to the basement to fetch firewood.

"The night your father died," said Ennemonde, "were you awake?"

"No," replied Alithéa.

"Did you see anything or hear anything?"

"No," said Alithéa.

Those nos were yeses.

Alithéa stopped writing. A short time afterward, she married an aging professor.

Life in the Swiss chalet was straightforward. It would be a mistake to imagine Samuel and Ferdinand dressing and acting like classic peasants; the same goes for Rachel. They weren't farmers but shepherds. The money their mother had earned during the war assured them complete independence, and having a skeleton in the closet is very beneficial for the mind. In addition, at the little fort where the two heroes had "sacrificed" themselves a monument had been put up, and Ennemonde had been given a medal. Rachel and her two brothers lived in perfect understanding. Samuel took care of purchases and sales, Ferdinand supervised the shepherds; he visited the pastures every day by jeep; Rachel minded the house and looked after their mother. Since that mother still weighed two hundred eighty pounds – pounds that were at this point far from firm – the brothers lent a hand when they were there; when they weren't, Siméon Wolf-Dog helped to settle Ennemonde in her armchair or to assist her in her various little bits of business. These four persons – Samuel, Ferdinand, Rachel, and Siméon – never uttered one word louder than another. The house seemed empty, while the chores appeared to get done by the workings of the Holy Spirit.

After Alithéa's marriage, Ennemonde developed an interest in the outside world. She had two of the Swiss chalet's windows enlarged: the one that looked east and the one that looked west; she had another, smaller window put in to the north, and a second to the south; she didn't count the glass-paneled door onto the south-east facing terrace. A wheelchair was bought. She'd regained a little strength in her wrists, and eventually she was able to wheel herself all alone from one window to the next, in the cold season; in summer she would even cross the threshold and go out onto the terrace. Her conscience clear, she regarded her world.

The sky is transparent, the air heady. The wind makes the sound of the sea in the fir trees. The grass bends, the lavender quivers. The tiles clink as if someone were walking on the roof. The wind makes the water tanks boom. The roads are smoking with dust, the beech trees shaking, the birches swaying, the poplars glittering; the wind runs through the grass like a fox. The arch of the walls makes a whistling sound. The latches dance against their keepers. The shutter hooks rattle; a stable door creaks. Wisps of straw blow about. The wind tumbles flocks of starlings the way a stream tumbles masses of serpentine. A crow is trapped in the middle of the sky, and calls out. It's already far away. It can no longer be heard. It vanishes. The wind has no thickness, yet it dims the afternoon light. All the sounds from upwind arrive pell-mell. Over that way, to the north, five or ten miles from the far side of the Jabron valley, there are flocks moving on Saint-Clerc Mountain; forests of firs that rumble around La Gloriette Rock; tractors plowing up former lavender fields on the slopes of Chanleduc; trucks straining up the hairpin bends of the Méouge gorges; mule trains toward Eagle Rock wearing neck bells that aren't of this region but probably from the valley of the Barcelonnette; the distant horn of the Marseille-Grenoble railroad snatched away at the moment when the lead car enters the level crossing of La Clapine (and so it's four o'clock – or sixteen hundred hours, if you prefer). The train is only audible when it passes that precise spot, and only when it's traveling in the direction of Sisteron and Laragne, because fifty yards before the crossing it emerges onto the plateau after a climb, its muzzle in the air, and its lowing is grabbed by the wind while it's still fresh and carried across the five mountains – Adret, Saint-Cirq, Rongnouse, Saint-Martin, and Pelegrine – to sound finally in the High Country; you need a good ear to make it out, or long practice; so then, people know that it's four o'clock – or sixteen hundred hours, if you prefer – though it doesn't make the slightest difference, since any man or woman with long practice couldn't care less about the hour! There are carts in motion down in the Jabron valley, but to make out exactly what they are, you need to be careful. The sounds don't arrive as they really are; the valley is very narrow, and to fetch the noise from deep down in there the wind has to drop all the way from the summit of Saint-Clerc, gathering up from the mountainside en route everything that's going on in Curel, where bells are ringing incessantly; at Bevons, where a construction company is bulldozing the earth to build terraces for orchards; at Miravail, where nine times out of ten in every season, except in the white of winter, they're gathering the flocks to count them. What can be heard of the carts in the valley, then, needs to be treated circumspectly. The more so because as the wind rises back up from the Jabron, already laden with everything mentioned above, it also rakes up and carries along all the sounds of the ubacs, in particular the extraordinary noises made by the boxwoods, the serviceberries, the white oaks, and the waterfalls, without mentioning that all that's needed is one motorbike climbing the Négron Pass for the indications to be completely distorted. It takes a really astute person to be able to tell whether it's one automobile or two, or the bus, going from Omergues to Noyers or in the opposite direction. Some can. Ennemonde can; she can even identify the make of the car, and hence the name of the owner. When the young schoolmistress of Saint-Vincent swapped her 2CV for a Renault, Ennemonde knew about it two days later. Ennemonde, and the shepherds who live in the open country, and the wanderers found in the High Country: woodcutters, charcoal burners, or romantic itinerants, sentimental transhumants, people with nothing better to do, who amble from north to south, from east to west, and all the diagonals, here eating a crust of bread, there gulping down a cup of coffee, here warming their hooves at a stove, there sleeping in hay, or straw, or simply in the cold and dark; all those people are equally good at telling the real from the false. They go further: they truly turn it into a profession, and ninety-nine percent of the time they make a living from it. Not only are they able to give meaning to the least pitter-patter borne on the wind – that's the schools letting out in Séderon; that's the moped of the guy who has the post office in Barret; that's the pulley in César Durand's barn at Ferrassières – they can also distinguish smells. Never mind that an aroma has passed over thousands of acres of flowering lavender, over bales of hay, over pinkish-red clover, over pits of liquid manure, over small towns with no sewers, over the latrines of building sites, over a hundred diesel carburetors – it's enough that someone is grilling a cutlet somewhere or other, for the wanderers to turn their steps toward the blessed spot from which the aroma comes. All the more when it's a matter of the sacred scraps that come from the slaughter of a pig. Especially because that always takes place in a week when there's a steady dry wind that's a little cool and lightly scented with the first flowers of the rosemary, and a burnished azure sky without the least trace of mist. When all these conditions come together, the wanderer, the transhumant, the handsome shadow who travels by moor, ridge, valley and plateau, is on the alert. He walks into the wind to steep himself in it, to breathe it in down to its smallest details. Previously, he's taken the precaution of descending as far as he can to the south so as to be downwind of as many farms, hamlets, and villages as possible. From there he tacks his way back up.

Almost always, now that the peasantry has become what's known as industrialized, the slaughterman – it's an aristocratic race – is precisely one of these roamers. When the animal reaches the desired weight, a courier is sent off into the open country in search of so-and-so, otherwise known as such-and-such. Once the man is found, he studies the weather, feels out the wind, looks at the moon, and picks a day. It goes without saying that his fellow wanderers know him for what he is. Without ever having been close to him – something that never happens among solitary individuals who are always several miles from one another – they know that so-and-so, also known as such-and-such, always carries with him a case containing knives; they've even occasionally heard him sharpening the knives on a gunflint: a characteristic sound passed on by the wind, its meaning unmistakable to someone whose sole concern is the quest for food. Someone who normally lives on snails that are often raw, white mushrooms that are always raw, and small game that's sometimes cooked – that person is immediately interested by the sound of knives being sharpened. He knows there's no point in following so-and-so, known as such-and-such – that that's the best way to lose him. So he drops as far as he can to the south and zigzags back upward into the wind.

On his way to the job, the slaughterman takes a thousand precautions (and God knows that God inspires precautions in these solitary types): after entering farms that are not his destination, he leaves them by the back door; sometimes he even sets out a day or two before his rendezvous so he has enough time to perfect his stratagems. For that reason, there's no point in following him. The folks who wander the plateau, without hearth or home, come from all social classes and from every category. There are bourgeois at odds with society; bankrupts; inconsolable widowers; younger sons kept from their inheritance; idlers, lots of idlers; eccentrics, extravagant men, bad men, petty criminals, anarchists, idealists, timid men, those simple in the head, or who are straight-out crazy. They don't harm anyone. They don't steal – not even those who were in the habit of stealing down in the Low Country. They rove. You meet them only rarely; when you do encounter one, he's frightening at first because of his gaze and his silence, but he passes you by. In the dead of winter, people take on one or another of them (even the crazy ones) at the farms, where they do odd jobs. Some of them, who are sort of like kings or emperors, never take refuge with the locals, whatever the weather. Where do they go on those fearful winter nights? That's their secret! There they are, spread out over forty square miles or more, little gods inhaling the wind in search of the smell of fat.

The slaughterman sets up in the farmyard. The creature to be sacrificed is brought out despite its cries. A strange thing: it's enough for the slaughterman to rub his knives one against the other for the pig to fall quiet, all at once. When he's a good slaughterman. But he's usually good, if he's been chosen from among the wanderers. Some farmers bring in a professional butcher. Professional butchers are not good slaughtermen. The animals don't accept the death they bring; they accept that brought by the wanderers. When a butcher comes to the farm, even if it's just a friendly visit, the pig shed, the sheepfold, even the stables erupt in uproar. The wanderer arrives with his knives, and all remains calm; there's merely a little moaning as the big moment approaches. If you seek to grasp what underlies this curious behavior, you realize that it's entirely a matter of ceremony; whether you're destined for sausage or for resurrection, death is the exact moment when all that is natural comes galloping back. Now, the butcher is pure technique: nothing counts for him except the relation between weight of flesh and weight of money. The wanderer comes in from the depth of the ages, he lives cheek by jowl with hunger. With him you can be sure the rites will be respected; and indeed, everything happens with admirable speed, ease, courtesy. The creature is already bleeding into the bucket, like a cask whose tap has simply been opened.

Afterward the body is washed with boiling water, scraped, rubbed, shaved, brushed, and pumiced. Then it's hung by the hind legs and disemboweled. The smell of the open belly drifts off into the wind. It's a smell replete with pathos. It's the smell that rises from battlefields, on the first day. There, it does the opposite job of that performed by military bands. By the same token, in these vastnesses that the mountains hoist up into the sky, the smell of the creature's insides, of its startled viscera, stopped in the very middle of their chemical operations, allows the solitary men to confirm the test they carry out every day. Hence comes an irresistible appetite, a frenzied need to feed the machine.

The fat is melted in a large cauldron. The smell arising from this procedure is filled with information. Depending on which wood is being burned, the name of the farm is proclaimed, or at the very least its location. Simple beechwood can give off a hundred different fragrances depending on whether it's dry, wet, covered in lichen on the side facing directly north, or gnawed at by the grub of the blister beetle; whether it's been cut into sticks or cubes; whether it was chopped beneath a full moon or a new moon; and so on and so forth, all the way to minute sub-tleties, such as for example the fact that it's been stacked in logs in the open air, or kept in the bakehouse, and above all whether it comes from a log cut according to the rules of the art, or one that's been chopped up any old how. Right away, everything is known from the smell.

These are only preliminary indications, but they're sufficient for the wanderer who has received and interpreted them to turn his steps to the north, the east, or the west (the south doesn't count; it's the direction by which the wind takes its leave).

Ennemonde goes even further in the interpretation of signs; she's as skillful as the wanderers at detecting the finest nuances. She knows just as well as they do the habits and constraints everyone has to conform to; that, for instance, at the Valigranes', nicknamed the Waterloos (no one knows why), the wood is always damp; that at the Martins' known as the Perussons (a kind of small wild pear) it's always dry, sometimes too dry; that at the Graniers' called the Marions (the name of one of their aunts, who was an easy woman), the woodpiles are marvels of architecture and marquetry, whereas at the Curbans', styled the Monkey's Asses (they have flattened noses), the wood is heaped slapdash. But she deciphers many other things in the wind. When the fat starts to melt, Ennemonde can give the last name and first name of the man, or more usually woman, who's stirring the cauldron with a skimmer. There's a smell of caramel that comes from not being vigorous in muddling the residue in the melting fat, and that is the exclusive style of Dorothée Dupuis of the Wheelbarrow Dupuis (as opposed to the Automobile Dupuis); if on the other hand a faint aroma of violet reaches her, that now is pure, unadulterated fat, white as snow, whose preparation has been entrusted to a master, and it can only be at the Martels', dubbed the Charleses (a souvenir of elementary school), because it's little Alexandre who's watching over the cauldron – a boy of twelve, but he already knows all there is to know about running a "household." Here, the word "household" means estate, in the sense given to the term between Clovis and Charlemagne: a vast arrangement of rustic crafts; a meaning still in use in the High Country and even the Low Country too. Before modern times set up an atomic center there, people would mention the "Cadarache household" as an example.

When the fat is completely melted and it's been poured into jars, at the bottom of the cauldron there remains a golden, lumpy, crispy coating that's called the *grignons*. It's this residue that the wanderers wish to claim, and their claim must be valid since it's taken into account. The grignons are dried off using a sieve, then they're scooped into a cone of newspaper that's given to the first wanderer to show his head over the wall of the farmyard. The next ones to come – there are sometimes two or three of them – have to make do with a little fricassee or a few inches of blood sausage.

Ennemonde is one of these wanderers, despite her complete paralysis, perhaps even because of it. She still has the memory of her deeds, of course; she tries to forget them, not because she regrets anything at all – on the contrary, she's proud as can be of what she's done and would do it again if needed – but she wants to forget it out of a kind of humility. It seems to her that after having so perfectly succeeded, it's important that she free herself of all pride, and render unto God that which is God's. Because without Him she could have been caught red-handed at least three times. For that reason she refuses to withdraw into herself, and instead she observes the world. The intelligence of her observations allows her to become part of that world; she engulfs herself in it, loses herself. It's the usual recourse of sinners (of those that conventional morality calls sinners): the more the sin is said to be "mortal," the more the world is material and helps the mind with its matter.

This is so true that at certain times, when she's done a proper mental accounting, Ennemonde sends Rachel to fetch a cone of grignons – as if she had need of them! She who has everything: hare if she wants it, thrush if she wishes (and she does), stuffed plovers simmered in terra-cotta pots, trout that Ferdinand catches for her in the Jabron, beef stew a hundred times better than what she ate at the table d'hôte (yet which she doesn't find to be better, even though it's simmered for a long time with pork rinds); she who has in her pig sheds over twenty pigs that are certainly fatter than the one slaughtered today at the farm of Joseph Négrel, a.k.a. Zulu, where the smell is coming from. And Rachel has no shame, Rachel understands that Ennemonde has a right to the grignons. And never mind that Joseph Négrel knows there are twenty pigs in Ennemonde's sheds; he'll give the cone of grignons to Rachel (if she's the first to arrive) because he knows that Ennemonde can claim it. He doesn't know the past, of course, but he begins from the fact that without well established rights, someone like Ennemonde would not come asking for grignons.

Like an aging queen, she delights in being rendered homage in this way, for no other reason than her looks, so to speak, and because she has seen men and women through and through and, since she's been immobile, she has learned to read winds, rains, storms, and sun. And it truly is as a queen that she appears up there on the terrace of her Swiss chalet, sitting in her armchair (on her throne, as she says, since it's a closestool), swathed in shawls and blankets or wearing her broad straw sombrero, depending on the season, smoking her Voltigeur cigars (for she's developed a fondness for them), carefully keeping track of all those who pass by, greeting them by their last name or first name, or nickname, or studying them in silence, sending puffs of cigar smoke in their direction; chatting, asking for a small favor, for example, to go pick three daisies for her in the meadow, or ten violets on the other side of the embankment behind the beech. Favors that aren't necessary – Rachel brings her daisies and violets when she really needs them – but that she asks of passersby she really likes, with the sole purpose of easing their conscience.

From the month of May they put her – or she puts herself, slowly turning the wheels of her wheelchair with her stiff hands – on the terrace that faces east. This direction is not the expected one, since only the south side offers shelter from the wind; but she's chosen the east, first of all because it's from that direction that the spring arrives, and also because on that side she can enjoy the cold northern light that she likes, and that reaches her at a slant. It might be thought that May is a little early to put a paralytic out on a terrace in a region where the first warmth of spring isn't felt until July 14th. But Ennemonde is encased in fat; she's a whale, she could withstand the cold of the North Pole. Plus, she has them wrap her in a shepherd's cloak with three collars and a hood, and she has a foot warmer filled with hot coals at her feet.

She's just spent the whole winter next to the kitchen stove.

Yes, the Swiss chalet's windows are broad and, safe inside, she can gaze out at sixty miles of snow, or sixty miles of midday shadows ground up in the wind. But it's the very fact of being safe inside that spoils her pleasure. Of course she has her family's passion for good things to eat, but it's not enough, or else the food doesn't suit her hunger. There hasn't been a letter from Alithéa since her wedding. In her case, for a long time Ennemonde has been observing with interest the victorious fight Alithéa is engaged in against mathematics. At that level, it's clearly akin to the combat that has to be fought against life, if a person wishes to live. These days, news of Alithéa comes only from the radio, the television, or the radical left-wing press, which sings her praises and prints her photograph every time she discovers that two and two do not make four. How did she end up over there on the left? Her husband was the one who pushed her in that direction. Unable to give her a child, he gave her ideas. What's the point of being so pretty! Did she really have to lumber herself with a spouse? With her numbers, she had everything she needed. Sacrificing your beauty while finding your happiness in numbers in which falsehood can only be unearthed with extreme cunning – that much is understandable; but to sacrifice your beautiful young days for some ambitious upstarts pushing in front of you is to waste your time at a game of four corners, and it's not terribly exciting to watch. The beverage maker of Carpentras is almost better. Now there's a woman who complicates her life, with her need for the romantic. She's just about to leave for her enchanted forest when the telephone rings: it's her banker informing her of huge profits on the most recent shares sold, the allocation of bonus shares, what you will! She has to turn back. Her Patrick and Ghislaine are self-satisfied dunces; having their adenoids removed made little difference. The beverage maker's husband is putting on weight in an ungainly manner; he bulges all over the place, which never happened to Ennemonde, who is three times as big as him, but whose skin always adapted with suppleness. Yes, it's much more interesting to wonder what on earth the beverage maker will be able to do in order to turn her accumulating capital into happiness. While here, around the Swiss chalet winter is raging with its coal-colored sky, its black snow as far as the eye can see, its savage winds. There's also Rachel. Every evening Siméon Wolf-Dog comes to see the woman he loves. This has been going on for ten years now. Whatever the weather, at the appointed time the door opens, the wind sweeps in and deposits Siméon Wolf-Dog in the kitchen. Gales, storms, tempests, cyclones: sound, o horns of perdition! He doesn't give a damn, he comes by. Strangely, he arrives on foot. He has three cars, two of them old, it's true, but still, three cars, counting the jeep he uses to take supplies to the shepherds, the Ford that's from '07 but still gleams, and a brand-new Peugeot. Fair enough, he might not want to get the Peugeot dirty (the roads are bad), but the Ford? And surely the jeep? After all, it's seven miles from Siméon's place to the Swiss chalet. Ennemonde suspected there was something going on here that was worth finding out about. Patiently, over two or three winters, she arranged it so she'd be alone for a moment with Siméon Wolf-Dog, and little by little, from one word to the next, she wormed it out of him. She was staggered! You should never despair for your children: look at Rachel, you can't say she's particularly beautiful, and yet do you know why Siméon Wolf-Dog comes on foot? Why he marches in the teeth of the wind across seven miles of dangerous paths, on a plateau where winter roars and rages? It's because taking the car would take so little time, it would be so easy, that he wouldn't feel he were coming to see the one he loves; whereas walking seven miles every evening, through the icy shadows, he can't forget that he's moving toward something precious, he has the time to be conscious of it and to relish it. And here he's been relishing it for ten years! What will become of Siméon Wolf-Dog? That's what Ennemonde asks herself. Clef-des-Coeurs ended at the makeshift machine-gun emplacement; it took airpower to finish him off. But Siméon Wolf-Dog? And Rachel – what will become of her? These are questions it's interesting to pose while winter is storming outside (often in absolute stillness) – a problem it's worth the effort to try to resolve while the snow falls and you can clearly see the blackness surrounding each snowflake. There isn't only one solution; there are a thousand. She contemplates all of them. She smacks her lips at them; but the winter is long.

And there comes a moment when she needs, not to imagine violence any longer, but to see it in action. So she places her stiff hands on the wheels and, engaging her entire strength, rolls herself all the way to the east-facing terrace. That's where the spring comes from. We're not talking about the spring of poets. In fact, it's not entirely clear, at this juncture, what use Ennemonde would have for flower-strewn meadows, birdsong, and suchlike twaddle. It's a real springtime that she needs. And that she has.

It's heralded by an inky blackness that stops up all the notches in the Alps. These are not clouds, it's the color of a sky wounded by the violence of the wind. For the moment it's slashing at the poplar groves of the Piedmont. It comes from Dalmatia; it's been frozen by the Adriatic and scorched by the sands of Ravenna. It batters the Alps. Turin flashes with sparks that fly from the streetcar cables knocking together.

The Dalmatian wind sweeps into the valley of the Suze and of Exiles; it's at Oulx, it's at Cézane, it bounces off Mount Tabor, Aigle Rouge, Chaberton, the slopes of Gondran; it howls as it chafes against the ridges of Pelvoux, it pounds the fir plantations of Le Lauzet, the larch forests of Orcières, it rakes the meadows of Mount Viso; it gorges itself on ice, snow, on avalanches in the strange wastelands that its yearly fury has baptized: Archinard, Estario, Pusterle, Viandre; and it finally emerges above Chorges.

At that moment, at the Swiss chalet Ennemonde has seen the sky darkening nearer and nearer, coming toward her. There's already a little something that interests her greatly, at the farthest point of the zenith, above her head – a sort of moan of the kind that's suppressed inwardly by living beings about to yield to their passion. She knows it well, this moan that no one else hears. Ennemonde watches Rachel, who's calmly going about her business, Samuel and Ferdinand, who go everywhere and do everything together, without whys or wherefores. She spares a thought for Alithéa and her "hair-splitting," her absurdly complex calculations; another for the beverage maker, and even one for the schoolmistress. They all imagine that night is coming, but something else is coming too! For the moment, all is quiet, it's still winter; but its conclusion has been announced. Nothing ends without upheaval, nothing begins without upheaval. That will be for tomorrow.

She calls, and they come and wheel her inside. Samuel and Ferdinand, who heard her voice, approach from in front of the house, kick their heavy shoes against the top step and go up to the kitchen, because it's time for them, with Rachel and Siméon Wolf-Dog (who'd be angry at himself if he missed the ceremony, though without knowing why), to get *la maman* ready for bed.

Four people is not too many for the job. The three men lift her and carry her to the trestle bed that Rachel has prepared. "Lift her and carry her" is much easier said than done. It's true that Samuel, or Ferdinand, or Siméon would each be capable on his own of lifting a dead weight of three hundred or three hundred ten pounds; but Ennemonde is not a dead weight, she's a living weight – living in her gaze (which is still so beautiful!), in her warmth, in her exact intelligence, which she's demonstrated numerous times throughout the day, and which can now be felt taking an interest in the fact that there are three men, two of whom are her sons, engaged in laying hands on her. This assemblage comprises much more than three hundred or three hundred ten pounds. They finally put her on the trestle bed. In the meantime, Rachel has emptied the pot contained in the throne. Siméon Wolf-Dog slips a pillow under Ennemonde's head, under the snow-white hair that is soft as silk. Siméon likes to touch her hair. Rachel washes it twice a month with some very expensive stuff that foams and that smells of violet (the only scent that Ennemonde likes, along with that of mignonette). It's thirty inches long and, when freshly washed, its suppleness makes it undulate like a snake. Very pretty hair, Siméon says to himself. When he first began "helping out," Siméon was not entrusted with important tasks; Samuel and Ferdinand reserved those for themselves. But then they saw it "brought pleasure" to Siméon, and so there was no more reason to keep him on the sidelines, and it was understood tacitly that the pillow under the head was his job, that taking off the slippers and stockings was Rachel of course, that reaching under Ennemonde's buttocks to untie her apron and unhook her skirt was for the hands of Samuel, Ferdinand, and Siméon together (six hands), that taking off the skirt, the apron, the pants, and the knitted woolen undergarments was Rachel once again, that propping up the belly, which at this point overflowed, was on the right side Siméon once again and on the left side Samuel once again, while Ferdinand took la maman's shoulders in his hands and lifted them so Rachel could take off the blouse; and so on and so forth.

The rest makes Siméon Wolf-Dog tremble ever so slightly – oh, not very much; he's seen worse; but it's a trembling in which he still can't clearly distinguish between what comes from terror and what comes from pleasure. First of all, it should be stated that Ennemonde is almost eighty years old, and that her eyes are still very beautiful – of course, at a certain moment they faded, when she wept so much, then they bloomed again when she began to occupy herself with the passions of her family – that the white of her hair is just as lovely as its black once was (which is rare); but that despite everything, eighty, as they say, is a fine old age, and it's never been known for bringing freshness and pulchritude to the flesh. It should be added that since Ennemonde has been immobilized (which is more than fifteen years now), this flesh has been increasing and growing lovelier every which way. So abundant is it, it gives the impression that if it were not manhandled into the frame and sides of the trestle bed, it would spill out onto the floor. Let it be said clearly: it no longer has a well-defined form. They know (the four of them that are there – Samuel, Ferdinand, Rachel, Siméon) that this is a woman because of the face and above all because of the first name; but as for finding it in the shape of the body, you could look and look: there's no indication. Now, to protect against the bedsores that could form in the folds of this flesh that is permanently unmoving, permanently depressed by its own weight, they will wash it, powder it with talc, and put on fresh underclothes every evening. After the skirts, the blouse, the undergarments, and especially a remarkable pair of Zouave pantaloons in madapolam, the three men and Rachel take off Ennemonde's day shirt. Now she is naked.

They wash her. She stops the one holding the sponge. (It's Samuel or Ferdinand, or Siméon, never Rachel, this was decided once and for all by their profound awareness of what they were doing.) "Wait a moment," says Ennemonde. She thinks she heard something new outside, but it was just the same moan as before at dusk, with nothing to indicate that a paroxysm is approaching. "Never mind, carry on."

After nightfall, you can no longer tell if a larger expanse of sky has been wounded. There's no sound outside except that inward moaning. It's still calm. It's still winter (so they think, at least), but it won't be for long now, and maybe even before they've finished washing her feet . . .

She's an old woman who is waiting for the spring. It'll come, of that there's no doubt; it'll be here one day or the next, soon. She's on the trestle bed. Shapeless, like a mixture of flour and water and salt, with a leaven of great freshness still, which is kneaded a little longer this evening but which tomorrow will be flattened out with the rolling pin to give it a usable form. Yes, the spring will come.

II

When mysteries are very crafty, they hide in the light; shadows are merely a decoy. The Camargue is a delta, the dumping ground of a large river, a recess. Up till this point it's been flowing, swiftly, without having the time to indulge in abstractions; it has lived. In this delta it's at its end, it's about to disappear into the sea, so it grows languid, it dawdles, it divides, it coils back on itself, it ruminates, hesitates, recapitulates; it examines everything that it's carried along up till now, mixes it together, makes it rot, glories in it.

It takes everything it's torn from its banks and makes silt and humus and sand out of it. Everything it's killed, it strives to resuscitate; all that is dead in it, it brings back to life. The seeds it has transported so furiously: here it pets them, coddles them, makes them burst forth.

If it had done this sooner, it would have been covered with greenery; but so soon before its disappearance into the sea, the climate can no longer be of help except to willows and marsh samphire; it's nothing but soda and salt by now.

Phantoms are the inhabitants of this broad daylight. A Camargue Hamlet would meet the ghost of his father at midday. After Christ, the religion of Christ is extolled by the sun. The sign of the cross is no longer enough to protect this vacillating region where the four elements mingle. What's needed here is a vacillation of signs, a multiplying of grounds for hope. Alongside the sacrificing of the just, there's a need of material for pleasure and adventure, and these are not so much the cardinal virtues that are associated with the cross, as they are sensualists and sailors. Here the cross is proud of what it has carried. The blood it has drunk does not make it feel ashamed; it lays claim to other blood; it has numerous feast days it can fill with its scent. The heart that is set up everywhere as a symbol very precisely represents the muscle and not the soul. Each clump of gorse exudes the odor of the charnel house; death wears the colors of the peacock. There are no longer any barriers between heaven and hell. The immortality of the soul is a clown making a face to entertain children; what bursts out and spreads in the light of day is the immortality of the flesh, the string of transformations, the wheel of life, the infinitude of adventures and avatars, the innumerable radiating paths of escape and of glory. The smell of decay that rises from roots and reeds is the smell of conquering warriors. In the place of faith and its tranquility, the shrines and plinths bear the sign of intelligence and of its battles.

In the sky of these gray lands whose colors have been worn threadbare by sun and salt, Lucifer-Athena twitters like a lark.

It goes without saying that a decent face is presented to the world. For anyone satisfied by superficial things, there is no problem: it's a piece of a *département*. It has its prefect and its police chief, its gendarmes and its fine citizens. It has its Masses and its pilgrimages like any Brittany or Auvergne, or Poland. It has its local government officials. It even has its own rituals; postcards and clichés do a tidy trade by them. If the sun put itself out for so little, there would be Camargues on the Atlantic coast. It's enough to widen the brim of a hat to pour Texan heroism into the tourists' hearts, but Dante only wears a cap.

In these broad flat spaces, the water moves where it will. It's no longer drawn by slope or weight but, so it seems, by desire. It has its boulevards, which it covers over with glints of light, and so it appears immobile. Only by being dazzled can you discern its quivering movement. It has its streets along which it passes, then it abandons them and the earth dries up and grows cracked like a heart. It has its ponds where it sleeps. It's no longer H_2O, it's Medusa. That noise of wind in the still air – it's the water, sounding as it slips through the reedbeds in search of a new path. It emerges onto open ground. Gray dust billows before its muzzle; it's a snake swelling and moving forward as it chews the earth. The sun coats it with black gold. Blind, yet laden with primitive strength, it rises, unfurls, metamorphosing before your eyes, with nary a thought for your Christian certainties, your political beliefs, or your scientific future; it drags along with it the components of illusions from which gods are spontaneously born. Even that which retreats slowly, retreats; even that which knows, knows only the escape routes.

It isn't that the water threatens you with a quick death. It's not deep; it's not fast. There's no need to step back: it will barely wet your feet. It doesn't threaten your soul. It will merely destroy your essence. Your order will become pandemonium; your physics and chemistry will turn into poetry. Where previously you depended upon Monsieur Eiffel, now you must rely on Monsieur Wave.

Often, in these reed-covered reaches of bronze, you hear the plashing walk of some unseen animal. You listen; words come to mind: Fox? Badger? Boar? None is satisfactory. Horse? Steer? Minotaur? The sound is at once weighty and light. Is it the winged lion of Assyrian reliefs? You look: the sky has whitened, the sun is by now offering only a gray light; the gorse bushes of the marsh seem plowed by some antediluvian form. The noise of the approach fills the entire space. The beast is so huge and unnameable that the day is made sick by it, the calendar curls up into itself. There's no more room: you feel as if you're gazing at an inner landscape; there's no more time: you're motionless, and you've been lying in wait for all eternity. The beast prowls; it's over there, it's here. It's in my heart, it's in the blackness of the swamp, it approaches, it moves away. It can't be seen, only its wake is visible. It's not searching for prey. (What could the flesh of a human mean to a beast of such consequence?) It's looking for a target, and you know you're the bull's-eye. The Andromeda complex opens a thousand icy avenues in the most home-loving soul. The odor rises: a smell of mud (we're in a delta), of fish, which speaks so vividly that the entire vast sky is nothing but the eye of the fish, and you imagine its scales rubbing against the galaxies, its tail reaching into the farthest distances of the world, spreading more rapidly than light. A smell of decay, though it's smooth to the mind, just as the smell of mushroom is smooth to the taste; a powerful smell of birth before form, at the hour when life mingled with death still has the right to choose what it will become. A smell of reptiles, of the first spinal columns, which were not yet capable of standing upright. A smell of all that had to be struggled against for thousands of years in order to reach the moment when you no longer touch the earth except with the soles of your feet. The mastodon you're waiting for seems wiser than all Churches put together. You're not afraid of its ferocity, you're afraid of its affection. It hasn't even shown itself yet, but already, by its sound and its suint, it has destroyed you and rebuilt you back to front, any old how, especially head over heels. People are afraid its form is contagious; they're frightened above all of not having a name for that form (which is going to be yours) and of being dragged (at my age! in my situation! in my family situation! with my job! being who I am!) into a truancy of the sensibilities. Nothing is more moving than the smell of shifting mud. Those reeds constantly swaying in the wake that's now approaching. The beast is about to break cover. The reeds part – it's coming! You face it with all the inhuman-ness you've been able to gather up within you (and that's a lot). Nothing emerges – except perhaps, high in the sky, an unseen body passing by. It moves away (while at the same time you feel embarrassed at the weapon you're holding in your hand) and heads off to be engulfed in the Mediterranean. To the south you hear clamorings upon the sea.

But there's a time when all grows calm. Clouds stretch out and turn red in the setting sun; they've fallen still on the hills beyond Nîmes and Uzès. They're already asleep. Here the current makes a quiet whistling sound. The shadows magnify anxiety, but romantic notions create orderly clearings in your fear. The ghosts depart along with the sun. A long green grasshopper carefully cocks the trigger of its thighs. It's evidently thinking about leaping. It kneads the dust with its tiny claws, turns its Philippe Auguste head in every direction, its antenna gauging the depth of the air; gathers its face between its knees, then finally jumps, opening its red wings, only to land in a place identical to that which it just left. Swarms of flies set widow's veils aflutter. Flights of mosquitoes dense as tigers sharpen their claws against the silk of the air. The diving of frogs adds another dimension to the evening's depth. The nighttime owl shakes its felt-like feathers in bush after bush. The nightjar hums. Somewhere a wading bird squeaks. This is also the time of the real fox, more invisible than its phantom; but it barks, and its domestic squabbles lend volume to the night. Rats flee rat dangers, chase rat prey, or dream rat dreams made up of gallopades, all in a pack, belly to the ground. The last daylight glints on the leading edge of a swallow's wing. The first star appears. The brazier of towns and villages lights up the curving horizon of the steppe. The broad branch of the Rhône can be heard muttering. Fish make snapping sounds on the smooth surfaces of the ponds. The melancholic call of herons bores into the night toward Aigues-Mortes. The silence has a Roman eloquence. Everything alive moves about soundlessly, even the reeds, even the stunted trees. Stars invade the delta. There are more constellations in the Vaccarès Lagoon than in the sky. The mud and the decay have the aroma of Turkish confectionery. Since love and throat-cutting emit the same cry, it sounds as if all matter is making love. The illusions of the night speak the language of the wet nurse. Horses are heard whinnying, cattle lowing, but it's unclear whether these animal sounds come from the land or from the sea, which is stirring its deep places and rubbing against its sands.

The red of the sun is still in Piedmont when the broadest dawn imaginable is quivering here; night has not yet left the alleyways of Arles when a snowy light, multiplied by long reaches of water and sand, lays its gleamings on the empty expanses. The sea itself is still dark. By Miramas and Salon, and around the Berre lagoon – where the land too is naked, where the water surfaces are broader and closer to the east – the dawn is still blue; here, reflected on the sands, it has instantly acquired an extraordinary whiteness. In Avignon the swallows are barely poking their bills out of their nests; here they wheel and squeak in the keen air. From the first rays of the sun, feathers burst forth on all sides: the black of the wagtail, the red of the stonechat, the yellow of the plover, the gray of the sandpiper, the green of the lapwing, the red of the godwit, the gray of the curlew, the white of the merganser, all the way to the orange shelduck, and the scoters that make their wheeling flights of woolen blue above the marshes. All that flies, all that trots, all that crawls, is roused to movement. While the sun scales the Alps to the east, a brief moment of life takes hold in the Camargue. Night, during which murders are carried out in half-sleep, flees toward the Cévennes; the African day that enflames the blood has not yet arrived. The mother boar quits its wallow with its young. All that's seen of these animals is the black stripe on their back; the rest of their coat is the color of the earth. Flights of waders cross the sky like maple seeds borne on the wind. The green lizard emerges from the hollows and moves forward across the sand with its somnambulist's gait: it runs full tilt or suddenly falls still, transfixed, for no reason. It's known as the quickfire or the *guillevert*. Some claim its bite is terrible; others say that it's Diana's companion and that it crawls across the chests of sleeping hunters to warn them of an approaching viper. It's the king of catalepsy: in the middle of a run, in the middle of a leap, it freezes and takes on the stillness of marble. Only its eye remains alive. When it fights, it's like a cat: it arches its back and rises on its paws, lowers its head, mutters silently, which is to say that instead of raising its voice, anger makes it utter threats in an ever-softer murmur, and it leaps upon its adversary in complete silence. It's so green that it seems the color green has just that moment been created especially for it. Zoologists say that it likes to assume a spectral attitude. The truth is that it sees the gods! The gods of this land are monsters. I don't mean that they're diplodocuses, merely that they cannot be understood by Cartesian reasoning. Christ, Buddha, Mohammad, and all the ophidians of the Aztecs, are nothing but the entrails of these immense deities.

The coronella or smooth snake leaves its hole. It's the most intelligent of the snakes. It too sees God with its tiny, blind-look-ing opaline eye, but more than that is needed to send it into a trance. It's Chinese; it spends its days writing ideograms in the sand.

And here's the warrior: the *zaménis*, or green whip snake, also known as the lash or the stingwolf because of its long slender tail. This snake is easily three to four feet or more in length. It's high-handed and enterprising; it climbs trees, plunders nests; it has a fierce, energetic character; it possesses a furious bite. The quickfire alone is capable of fighting back, leaping at its throat and driving it away. Others it swallows alive, naked and raw. It likes to feel its prey struggle and slowly die, even feel it scratch against its expandable gullet. It revels in the agony of others. It likes not just to feed itself but to relish the process. It has no use for that which is inert, but as soon as it sees some living thing in the vicinity, it thinks (for it does think) how exquisite it would be to digest that life. It's a political creature. Its digestion is Caesarean. It has two penises equipped with backward-curving barbs that, once it attaches itself, make separation difficult, often tragic. The female can only either die or kill the male and eat him (which nine times out of ten she prefers to do).

Much needs to be said about snakes. There are the two great serpents of the river, which enlace this land. There are marshes, mudflats, sands, tangles of floating vegetation, the ghastly heat, the blinding light, the invisible gods. It is the geometric place of the snake.

At this time, as the sun is still inching its way up the eastern slopes of the Alps, all that crawls, all that leaps, makes the most of the white light of dawn. It's a moment of splendor. These creatures, glorying in their feathers, their coats, their scales, do not yet exist; for now they're merely set in motion by their essence.

The ringed snake or lady's snake: large head, short muzzle, big eyes, round pupil, yellow iris: an eye that seems to emit light, as if the rest of the world were the eye, and this eye the spectacle. The female, the one most often seen, is a big lump of a thing: she's three feet long (on average; in some cases she can grow up to six feet and more); she's fat; she doesn't crawl in decipherable ideograms like the green whip snake: she drags herself along. She's not a learned lady but a housewife. Her mate is slim and smaller; no one would think they were of the same species. He fidgets; he's a kind of olive green, sometimes blue; he wears the Order of the Golden Fleece: an orange triangle suspended from a white necklace. The ringed snake doesn't bite, hence its alternative name. But it frightens with its girth, its muscles, its ferocious appearance, its eye that rejects the spectacle of the world and considers itself the spectacle of the world. People believe that's why it doesn't bite. On the other hand, the lady's snake has a habit of spraying anything that seizes it copiously with its feces and a foul-smelling secretion from its cloacal glands. Such aggressors are rare. The ringed snake is huge and has no difficulty looking fierce. It ingests its prey starting with their hind parts, to leave them all the time in the world to scream. It savors these screams. Despite its weight, it's a beautiful animal in the morning when it isn't yet engaged in the hunt and is enjoying its own beauty. It's seen in avenues that the waters have abandoned, or at the borders of the marshes in the first patches of mud. It's never stoned, because no one can hope to kill it with a rock. It's put to death with a stick or a shotgun. Snakes, of whatever kind, have such a simple and utter beauty that men derive pleasure from killing them.

Since we're speaking of beauty, let's go back to the birds. There are thousands of them, of every kind, every plumage, every color. There's not a single lost islet in the distant Atlantic that does not delegate here one of its gannets, or a black-headed gull or little gull, a sea swallow or Sandwich tern. The cormorant, the red-breasted merganser, the oldsquaw, the diver, the lapwing, the stint, the turnstone, and the sandpiper, all mingle in a thousand kinds of flight – red, green, blue, yellow, orange, black, pure white, and that iris gray which all other colors turn into. All the way to the bird of paradise known as the western parotia, which has three slim, extraordinarily long plumes on either side of its head, and on its flanks a lovely emerald-green glaze, and which comes here acting the musketeer, twirling its mustache. Some of the birds supposedly only inhabit some remote Siberia: they are here. Others, like the golden-headed trogon or the blue cotinga, have need of savannahs and broad alligator-infested rivers, yet here they are in this land of bare sands, gorse bushes, and small lizards. There's even the turaco, a sort of phoenix – a red bird that loses its color in water. If the turaco gets wet and rubs itself against the sand, the sand turns red and the turaco becomes white; but as soon as it dries, it regains its color. This no longer happens with the bird's dead, dried body. There are swifts, quail, cranes, storks, geese, a thousand varieties of ducks, all migrants and travelers, who come here to molt and refresh their plumage. There are those that originate in forests, colored from darkest black to brightest red; there are birds of the steppe, birds from the banks of the Lena, birds from the banks of the Amu Darya, birds of the Euphrates, birds of the Silk Road, birds from the Kerguelen Islands and from Newfoundland. In colonies of several hundred you can find the finch of Punta Arenas; the Magellanic grouse turns in the pure blue of the sky, just as it turns frantically in the storms and strife of the Beagle Channel. The Eskimo curlew is found alongside the desert wheatear. The tanagers and marsh birds of the Americas build their nests here in the shape of an alembic, the way they make them in the tropics, to protect their offspring from climbing mammals. Some hollows in dunes conceal simultaneously the nest of the Sahel paradise whydah, which never contains eggs, and that of the highland guan, which brims with them. And there are indigenous kinds, folks from here – the rank and file that haunt the thatched roofs and tiled eaves from Carpentras to Montpellier, from Sète to Marseille, from Vauvert to Lambesc: the cuckoo, the greenfinch, the great tit, the coal tit, the wagtail, the oxpecker. . . The finch, the blackbird, the thrush, the nightingale, the goldfinch, the bullfinch, the lark, the robin, the magpie and, finally, the sparrow, the good Gaulish sparrow, the laziest of birds, which lives in the company of humans, abounds in towns and cities, and here maintains its idle urban habits.

All these foreigners and locals mingle in flight and in their morning calls. Every throat harmoniously swallows and expels the air that tastes of mystery and marsh. Those whose windpipes are cylindrical emit the sounds of the flute, the fife, the recorder; those who have a cone-shaped windpipe, narrower toward the bottom than at the top, buzz like organ pipes. Some produce the sound of horns, or trumpets, or trombones; others hammer on crystal strings or make drums vibrate. The canary, the greenfinch, the oriole sing their love. The sparrows send up a doleful clamor at the sight of a shrike. The sparrowhawk and the buzzard utter shrill cries at the partridges. Everywhere the air resounds with whistles and clucks of tenderness or unease. The warbler raises a voice that gives the nightingale a run for its money. The songbirds intone their distinctive melody of war and of terror; the guttural voice of the bullfinch taps against the smooth surface of the ponds with such force it makes them tremble; the carnivorous birds with slenderer beaks sigh more gently than any other; their tones are more passionate, more enchanting, as they keep watch around themselves with the extreme animation of their cruel, unintelligent eyes. The noisy birds of the open spaces, which have evolved to be able to call to one another across large distances over the sound of the waves, stir the far-flung gorse bushes and the stagnant waters with their heavy wings and their hullabaloo.

Finally, in a single stroke, from the top of the Alps the sun leaps into the delta. All at once, everything falls silent, all flights cease, the birds all scurry into the bushes, go to ground beneath tufts of spurge, slip beneath the gorse, drop anchor on the darkest of the marshes. For a moment all the water surfaces seethe with the glinting of every wing, are streaked with the wakes of all the flotillas as they scarper; then once again they become smooth and empty like a mirror in which only the bare sky is to be seen. Silence. Now, along with the daylight the secretary bird enters the stage. He comes in with rapid steps: that's why he's also called the messenger bird; he has his quill tucked behind his ear like a bookkeeper, which is where he gets his name. In order to walk even faster, he uses not his wings but his ferocity, which he hardens like a lead sinker in his forward-leaning head; in this manner he drives himself onward like a Greek hero. He paces the sands like Achilles circling Troy. He's a walking vulture destined to live in deserts. His life is pure Iliad. He has greaves on his shins. He's gray as an ancient warrior, except on his flanks, where, like old trophies of plunder, he wears emerald, sapphire, and tarnished gold. For a long time now he's been on the lookout for snakes – watching for the largest of them. He was waiting for the sun. The sun is here; he waits no longer, he attacks. It's usually a big ringed snake, thick as a man's arm, that stops, holds its head up, puffs out its neck and whistles fearsomely. In the nearby bushes every-thing crouches down and hides. The secretary bird extends one of his wings, brings it in front of himself like a shield, and covers his legs. The snake darts forward; the bird leaps, strikes, springs back, jumps in every direction, and returns to the combat, still presenting his feather buckler; and while the snake exhausts itself trying to lunge at that soft gray smock and bite it, the bird swipes it away with vigorous blows of his other wing. The rep-tile reels and tries to flee. The secretary bird smashes its head with his beak and drinks its brains; around the still-twitching cadaver he performs a little ritualistic hopping dance, beating his wings, nodding his head with a shake like a horse doing the Spanish walk; finally he tears his victim to pieces and swallows it in large chunks. Sated, he closes his eyes as if asleep, motion-less, drunk from eating, from gratified ferociousness, from logic.

* * * *

If I've spoken of theater, it's because we're part of an all-round dramaturgy, as in every sun-drenched land. Beneath the accu-mulated silt of the river, the bone structure of former glacial moraines lifts little islands of firm ground above the marshes and the submersible lands. On these islets people have built small white houses with thatched or tile roofs such as are found in all deltas and estuaries, at the mouth of the Guadalquivir just the same as at that of the Odiel or the Río Tinto. These houses look for all the world like sugar cubes; everything about them suggests isolated dwellings for a single occupant. I'll say even more precisely: a single man. This architecture (simplicity in the extreme: four walls whitewashed inside and out, and a roof) speaks neither of woman nor of family. Nor hearth – it's the complete opposite of the English notion of home. It is not a matter, as in rainy lands, of lingering amid the smells of married life. The only luxury here is shade and the siesta. The four walls and the roof make the shade; that is all that's asked of them (and the siesta's in the bag). Actually they're asked for a little more, like anywhere in fact, but whereas in lands of continual twilight people need both to have a hearth and to make it lovely, here they're content to paint the walls pure white, brilliant white, so that, in the dazzlement produced by that white, the shade seems even darker. And that is enough, precisely because of the theater that the sun offers at every crossroads of the senses.

An immediate theater, based on blood – and on violence, since that is the most direct way to obtain blood. Lands where the light is gray have an extended sense of time that makes possible the generative patience of diplomacy and, as a result, of society; sun-soaked lands live at a fast pace, making violence and solitude necessary. This speed of life produces a lie. Not the opposite of truth, but a generalized lie, in other words, the creation of another reality.

This is the human condition of the inhabitants of these little sugar-cube houses. In this age in which people make money from everything, even (and especially) from appearances, we ought to distinguish between authentic inhabitants, of whom there are very few (and they're almost invisible), and artificial ones, of whom there are many (and they are very much in evidence).

I once knew one of these authentic Camarguais. He was a man who did not look picturesque. He didn't have a large hat or a meticulously knotted scarf; he didn't wear cowboy boots; he didn't know how to pose in front of a camera, and when he laughed he exposed a toothless mouth (from raw leek, not from garlic – which is no better, by the way). He was not alluring. He talked exactly like everyone else, which is to say, French with a strong Southern accent. He was such a marvelous horseman that in an armchair he cut a sorry, bumpkin-like figure. In the saddle he brought to mind not the admirable lawmen of the West, nor circus riders, but a sort of equestrian proletariat; on his horse he was like a workman at his workbench. He did not ride for appearance's sake, nor to charm; he rode for himself, and to look after his cattle. He wasn't concerned about an audience, he was concerned about his buttocks. Since he had a precise job to do, and this job required him to be on horseback twelve hours a day, and he'd been doing it for more than thirty years, he'd adopted not the most elegant way of sitting in the saddle, but the most comfortable.

He had a cap (like everyone else), an old woolen jacket (a double-breasted coat in blue worsted that had been worn for Sunday best in 1913), long pants, and espadrilles. He also had a decent little belly, of the sort they call a brioche, and a tobacco-chewing habit that did not improve his breath.

As for his authenticity, no one could question it. He was the last in a long line of ancestors, all bachelors, who had all lived at Mas-Thibert or thereabouts. Solitary men live their solitude in the shade of a carefully tended family tree. My authentic Camarguais was called Louis, had no last name or claimed to have none, and could go back as far as his great-grandfather. The birth of that distant forebear, in turn, was lost in the mists of time. The only thing known for sure was that in 1823 he'd been a cowherd for a man named Adolphe Émeric, and on the land where he minded the cattle he had built the sugar-cube house that Louis still occupied in 1959. Along with the house, there was another relic of this character whom Louis called the "old man": it was a little French tricolor flag with an embroidered motto that read "Liberty or Death." A relic from the coup d'état of 1851. In that year the "old man," who according to what Louis said must have been sixty or sixty-five years old, had found near a place called Wild Man's Ferry a small body half hidden in the gorse. Dragging him out of the marsh, he recognized the butcher boy from Bellegarde, and saw that he was still breathing, despite his nostrils being blocked up with mud. He cleared the kid's nose, carried him to his cabin, and took care of him. The little butcher's body was wrapped in this flag. When he was able to speak (which happened fairly quickly, because he very much wanted to), he told the old man that, as a member of the republican insurgents, he had been chased by the soldiers; he'd attempted to swim across a branch of the Rhône but, carried away by the current, he'd run out of strength and eventually had lost consciousness. The old man brought the butcher boy back to the land of the living, and the rebel left his flag at the cowherd's. Wild Man's Ferry was a cable ferry operated by one of those muscle-bound invalids who have been the delight of Romantics since Quasimodo. This one was neither hunchbacked nor one-eyed, but still he wore rolled-up sleeves and had corkscrew shoulders. Nothing hinted at his strength, yet he was strong as an ox. He lived, not far from the place where the old man had found the little butcher, in a house that also looked like a sugar cube, but was concealed in a grove of green canes.

The butcher boy had puzzled the simple mind of the cowherd, in particular presenting this problem: How do people lucky enough to have a job as interesting as that of butcher, end up trying to cross the Rhône with a tricolor flag wrapped around their body?

It was unsolvable; and to convince himself of this fact (and also to revisit the scene of his exploits), the old man often lingered around the ferry.

Now, our aquatic Quasimodo had a daughter who was as Quasimodo-esque as himself. She was around thirty-five or forty years old and, for more than twenty years, despite the strange build of her body, and thanks to the kind of milky flesh that always attracts strong men, she had charmed the leisure-time of all those worth the effort, from Port-Saint-Louis-du-Rhône to Le Grau-du-Roi. She'd had a string of children who, when their time came, drowned, died of croup, choked on cherries, or barely survived, fishing for frogs, swimming like tunnies and so on. Though aware of these things, the old man had never seen this dream creature up close. Now he did. It was May. For Carnival of the following year, as they were sounding the trumpets for Ash Wednesday, the ferry girl brought him a little boy, all new, and not at all unshapely. According to her, he was their son; according to him, it was possible. This one here, she added, she didn't want to put him in the regular flock, because he had red hair. (The down on his head did in fact look red.) The old man never went against natural things, and this desire seemed natural to him. He took care of the child, which is to say he laid him on sacks in the corner of his shack and, the rest of the time, he carried on minding the cattle on horseback. But when he came back (sometimes after ten hours of riding through storms) he would always find the little one clean, fed, and smiling, or bellowing like a calf, but purely for the pleasure of it. So it was, till he was two or three (though three years old is already a lot) – until the day when the ferry girl was blown to pieces by a full box of gunpowder with which she'd been fishing, right beneath the Beaucaire bridge, in the company, as it happened, of a Gypsy she'd been pleasuring on the sly. For the old man, this premature explosion opened up a path to emotion. When he'd seen the child being looked after by mysterious hands, he hadn't thought it was the Holy Spirit; the moment he learned about the Beaucaire accident, he looked at the boy's mouth and said to himself: "It's my job to fill it now." The boy's hair was not red at all (nor was the old man's, in fact); he'd known this from the very first days (he wasn't born yesterday; the hair had been dyed with birds' feathers; but it was precisely this ruse on the part of the mother that led the old man to think this actually was his son – without going too far, however, for the old man was never one to go too far). He had called his horse Bicou; he called his son Bicou, and come what may.

The winter of 1875 was atrocious. Such cold had never been known before. The mistral kept up continuously; you could barely stick your nose out of doors. The old man rode all the more in search of animals that were drunk on the cold and had gone off to wait for death among the dunes. The ponds froze in an instant around the feet of the ducks; to hunt them you only had to break the ice. Like all men of the sun, the old man yielded to the seductive temptation of the cold. He evidently preferred death to life, and, after coughing a great deal (with a cough that curiously resembled the melancholic sound of cattle lost in the night), he lay stiff and silent on his cot.

Bicou was twelve years old. For the preceding week, he'd looked after the herd all on his own. Within two weeks of the old man's death, while the body was mummifying from the cold in the house, which had been closed up like a tomb and which Bicou no longer entered, the herd was being handled masterfully by the child. The owner (who had changed – it was no longer Adolphe Émeric, who was now "deceased," but his oldest child Jules, who'd had all sorts of problems dividing up the estate with his sisters and brothers-in-law) – the owner of the herd, then, only found out about the death of the old man in July. At that point Bicou had long since abandoned the hollow in the grass where he'd slept, and had once again opened the door of the little sugar-cube house; he had long ago buried in the sand the carcass of the old man, which swarms of bees had tidily emptied and cleaned. Jules Émeric sent a man from Vauvert to tend the cattle. This man arrived on Wednesday morning; on Wednesday evening his horse returned alone to Mas-Thibert. The man from Vauvert was found, alive but dazed, having been knocked senseless, lying flat as a pancake across a doorway. He didn't know what had happened to him. He had a hole in the back of his head, likely made by a rock. He must have injured himself falling from his horse. Jules Émeric sent a man from Lunel. The man from Lunel's horse came back alone and the man from Lunel was found alive but dazed, having been knocked senseless, lying flat as a pancake across a doorway. And as for what had happened to him? Nothing. According to him, nothing had happened. He'd heard the buzzing of a large fly. He too had a hole in the back of his head. Jules Émeric sent a guy from Nîmes. This one, forewarned, was on his guard. So much so that he was found, flat out, just like the others. The inhabitants of Nîmes being renowned for their intelligence, people listened to what this man said. He said that in his opinion, in those parts a slingshot was being expertly employed. Jules Émeric put Bicou in charge of the herd. He'd seen that the cattle obeyed the child's voice as one; he thought to himself that, aside from anything, a child is paid much less than a man; and since this child had a slingshot, such a fact simply needed to be taken into account.

Whether truly out of heredity, or from habit developed over long years of living together, Bicou closely resembled the old man in character. Nothing came before the herd, or more exactly, nothing came before the pleasure of living on horseback behind the cattle. But from his mother he'd inherited a taste for certain embellishments — skill with a slingshot was one; a need for company was another. It was less a matter of human company than company in general, and especially in the period of puberty and adolescence, Bicou confined himself to the society of cattle, birds, small mammals, reeds (above all when the marsh quivered in the evening wind), and even minerals. He knew that you never get bored, even with a piece of granite, if you force yourself to study it for hours on end. As for meeting people, spending time with them the way he spent time with granite and with wild creatures – he wasn't against it in principle, and he gave it a try a little later; but, without the least metaphysics of course, he found such company less agreeable than the other. His maternal grandfather had bequeathed him a Herculean strength, which people were constantly wanting to test; he didn't like to be the center of attention, his whole way of life led him to be a spectator, and there was nothing to see in other people. When, after his way, he studied a man or a woman for a long time, not only did he not learn much from it, but the object of his attention ended up getting mad and making fun of him.

This need for both solitude and company made him adept in the craft of basketry. When he was weaving wicker, he felt as if he were managing masterfully in some society and bending it to his will. The great moral satisfaction he drew from this occupation led him to create novel forms of basket weaving. With his fingers he had audacious turns of eloquence, insinuations, supplenesses; he was the Cicero of the basket. In this way, while he remained silent his words traveled the region. Carried away by this manner of expressing himself, he perfected it at every moment of his life. He knew all the resources of this land; his long horseback rides with the cattle, his power of consultation with all that existed, animal, vegetable, and mineral, gave him access to an extraordinary library of dictionaries of expression. He knew where to find thorny restharrow, which was used to make a gold-colored dye; sea bindweed and sea kale, whose sap, mixed with salt, stands in for crimson; the herbaceous starwort, round-leaved wintergreen, and bog myrtle, which, when ground together with mussel shell, produce the perfect black. He'd learned to use colors sparingly, to fix them with hedgehog gall, to tell the age of a willow and to choose branches whose fibers were supple enough to permit him a range of means in a grand style, offering many personal joys; he knew how to varnish his work with a concoction made of false fleabane, otherwise known as Saint Roch grass. In a word, through a particular sort of irony, by simply following his own path he had made himself desirable.

One evening upon coming home he found, unhitched in front of his house, what was known in Lunel, Aigues-Mortes,

Saint-Gilles, Vauvert, and even Nîmes, as the coach. It was a gilded wagon whose rear part rose to form a platform like those on the small boats used in water jousting. This platform was hung with red and encircled by a balustrade in fake marble of the "garden of love" variety; hanging from the balustrade, like seaweed on Thetis's chariot, were two hunting horns, two trombones, and a cornet. The drum was not in sight. This vehicle went from town to village to farm, transporting a personage that some called Casagrande, others Diablon; he was a Gypsy. He pulled teeth to the sound of a band. To this art he added the manufacture of worm powder; he stole chickens, cast vague spells, and in addition he was a basket maker. Or if not him, then at least his wives; he had seven of them, of whom two were always pregnant at any given time; those two were assigned to do card readings. The throng of children played the horns and performed drumrolls to drown the cries of the patients; the girls sold the baskets, along with allegedly handmade lace that came from the factories of Nancy. Casagrande, of indeterminate age, lean, dark, gleaming, had a handlebar mustache, which rendered all the folds of his mouth definitively bitter, even when he smiled.

Casagrande believed he had need of diplomacy to learn

Bicou's secrets and had laid his plans accordingly. As head of his tribe, he'd decided to employ the charms of his youngest wife, with whom, as it happens, he was not on good terms. This young woman, named Myriam, in whose blood various Macedonias and Balkans mingled, had only accepted Casagrande's yoke in obedience to the extravagant laws of her race; in reality she was aiming at something higher than a puller of teeth, without knowing exactly what, and she was looking about for points of comparison so as to orient her future with full knowledge of the facts. By chance, this particular year she was not pregnant, and given her character she was in danger of not being so for a long time. This was not the moment to hesitate; Casagrande did not, and before setting up by Bicou's white shack, Myriam had been given a long lecture with the aid of the riding crop that was used on the mule. She was all set.

But there was no need, because Bicou, like all great orators, was never one to make a mystery of his methods. All the same, he appreciated Myriam, or, more precisely, in revenge for the riding crop, Myriam did everything to make herself be appreciated.

Casagrande remained for three years next to the little sugar-cube house. From time to time he would go off to extract teeth and sell (what was now) luxury basket ware; then he would come back. Bicou's secrets were a gold mine, and they were numberless. Then, one fine day Casagrande left. He would return no more.

Bicou knew it: the day before, one of his knives had been stolen, which is always the sign of a permanently broken contract. For him it was child's play to catch up with the coach before it reached the Beaucaire bridge. He made them give him the little girl who Myriam had had in the course of those three years. He was insulted in the usual manner, his manhood cast in doubt, but they gave him the child. Before crossing the river, Myriam gave Bicou to understand that she herself had stolen the knife expressly to alert him. She'd never forgiven Casagrande the whip blows, especially from a mule crop, and she was delighted to see escape from his clutches a girl who in a few years could have served various ends.

For Bicou she served as sheet anchor. Three years of rubbing shoulders with the tribe from the coach had caused him to lose his taste for minerals, vegetables, and even animals. In the strong smell of those females and their horde of children there were alcoholic fumes that made you dizzy; in Casagrande there was everything that people in villages look for in bezique on Sundays. In memory of this woman, then, who had embodied all of the above, and who in addition had on certain occasions cooed like a dove, he called the little girl Myriam.

Myriam had in abundance all that which makes men: a rough life and broad horizons, silence and natural laws, desires and solitude; but she remained a woman. She was no beauty; her mother hadn't been either; her father was like everyone; so. . . But health had not been given to her sparingly. By force of circumstance, she dressed as a man up to the age of thirty: where would she have found skirts at the start of her life? They had to make use of Bicou's old pants; afterward she got used to it; after that, she dressed as a woman because she had Louis.

She had Louis on purpose, the way you purchase an essential need. When she counted up, she found that she'd spent more than twenty years with her backside in the saddle, which gives a woman a good seat, spares her from a certain turbulence, and generally speaking directs her toward accomplishments.

But we're getting ahead of ourselves: Bicou had a royal death. One evening he did not come home. Myriam, who at that time was twenty-five, found a large gathering of cattle at the place known as La Jouquelle. It was the middle of the night. Myriam was riding a white mare that was thrown into panic but quickly brought back to reason. Its flanks and mouth flecked with blood, the horse came at an angle, resistingly, toward this huge herd, blacker than the night, from the midst of which came a low singsong murmur, like the purring of a cat half a mile wide. There were cattle there that did not know Myriam, but the ones that did came to meet her and, escorting her on either side, led her like a Caesar into the holiest of holies of the assembly. Gripped between her iron-strong thighs, the mare did not flinch. Myriam had a storm lantern hanging from the saddletree.

It was in the midst of this throng (by the red light of the lantern), before a hundred cattle, that she found her father dead. She brought him home, followed by all the cattle; they broke up their cortege as they drew close to human habitations. Bicou had no wound, but his face was purple, and his tongue stuck out like that of a hanged man. He had quite simply been touched by the finger of God, which in the medical language of our day is known as myocardial infarction; but I'm talking about the viewpoint of Sirius.

The owner of the herd (no longer Émeric – he had sold it to a townsman of Marsillargues) took the news in stride and left the herd in the care of the "young man." He did not know Myriam was a woman. She too was unaware of it.

She learned it, not the way people usually do, but from the meaning that she gave to her solitude. She had no desire to weave wicker. She tried, just as she'd tried when her father was still alive, but having only herself to please now, she did not succeed. She lingered in the company of the heifers, but she was too wise to share their melancholy.

One autumn evening, when the animals had settled down, she saddled a fresh horse for a run, and at five o'clock she was in the cypress fields over by Cavaillon. She laid her plan, sized things up, made numerous calculations in the blink of an eye. For six francs she bought a skirt and a blouse at a grocer's-cum-hosiery in Plan d'Orgon and went back home.

During that autumn she made the same journey several times. She roped her horse to the darkest of the cypresses, put on women's clothing in a cane thicket, and went to show herself at a fruit and vegetable farm. She'd chosen a time when the males of the region are idle, and smoke their lugubrious cigarettes along the road as they kick at rocks. She came to an arrangement with one of them, a laborer who'd looked amiable to her since he was no longer young and had many hairs on his face. She'd chosen well, because he showed no surprise, but he asked for forty francs. Nothing could have reassured Myriam more; that was exactly how she'd understood the matter; but she didn't have forty francs. (It was a very large sum.) She promised to come back; he promised to wait.

And wait he did; he waited for more than a month while Myriam, dressed as a boy, combed the markets and fairs in quest of her forty francs. At each little village, hamlet, or even large cattle farm, they "ran the cattle." This involved picking out young animals that were whole and hot-blooded, sticking a rosette between their horns, and promising five francs, sometimes six, to whoever could retrieve the rosette. The animals played the game, though they did it the way animals do, striking with their horns; the men played it with tricks, agility, and boldness.

To this game Myriam brought in addition that which she'd learned from her father: charm. Not of posture or grace – the young men were a thousand times more agile than she was – but a kind of "cattle language" that she murmured as she approached the creature. In this way she gathered together ten, twenty, then thirty francs. She had some difficulty going from thirty to forty: autumn was ending, and along with it the fairs. There was one last one, at which they let loose the worst cattle in all creation. Myriam, who did not for anything in the world wish to ask for concessions, left herself more open than usual and almost got herself killed. Her courage – the spectators were unaware where it came from – was cheered by all.

She saw things through, then; but she didn't inform her boss till after the birth of the child (which she named Louis). The townsman of Marsillargues threw his hands to the heavens when he saw his cattleman in skirts. He had to be shown the child, and even see it being suckled, to be convinced. He raised his arms skyward once more and brought in a guy from Arles to mind the herd.

The guy from Arles played with the child. A few months later, he played with the mother too, though this time it was entirely different from the business with the forty francs. And as it happened, Louis never had any brothers or sisters.

In 1944 Louis came out of prison. He'd been put away for two months for some nonsense; he was innocent, though it had taken him two months to realize it. Any smart man would have figured it out sooner. But Louis was not especially liked in the delta. He wasn't the only one: he was one of that category of citizens attached to tradition. Now there are various kinds of traditions, or in any case two: real ones and false ones. There are traditions that arise from the need to live, and traditions that arise from the need to appear. Those who practice the second kind don't like those who practice the first; and in general the second group are craftier.

In fact, my Louis didn't make a big deal of it. He didn't act like some kind of Silvio Pellico; he'd eaten his beans and lentils with gusto, he climbed back in the saddle like a sack of dirty laundry, and he left, trotting across his wilderness, which wasn't quite so deserted as once, but Louis knew many places that still were.

Louis took after his grandfather Bicou and his mother; he must also have had something of that forty-franc father Myriam alone had known. If you thought about it, with his physical strength he also took after the Quasimodo. It has to be said that this strength was not in evidence and that Louis would never, even in his lovely youth, have passed for an Apollo of the beaches, but. . . But he could tear a pack of thirty-two cards with his bare hands, which in itself is not too shoddy. It was a strength he never used, except to stop his horse by tightening his thighs, or to bring order to the herd. He measured himself against cattle, never against men. Quasimodo's strength, combined with the liveliness of body that had distinguished the first Myriam, worked wonders during Louis's adolescence.

He seemed to have been marked by the arduous tasks his mother had imposed upon herself to bring him into the world.

The fashion for enclosures where people confronted cattle with rosettes between their horns had spread to the point that, with a little maneuvering, it could pass for a tradition. All around the Mediterranean there are those who wish to follow their roots back to Minos; having a little Minotaur in the blood is a convenient thing for a life of idleness. Since there was idleness pretty much everywhere, this kind of nobility, which dispensed with the need to trace things back to the Crusades, was attractive to many. The "cattle pen" became a sort of fashion for a sizable public eager for exotic entertainments bearing the stamp of approval of the State, which is to say Homer, for this was a state of mind. These events, which previously had been put on by simple peasants looking for a distraction, were now run by licensed organizers. At the time of Louis's adolescence, there had still been pure contests in which everyone joined in the fun; now, more and more it was a show presented by professionals in front of a sitting public (who had paid for their seats).

More and more, people who'd grown used to having the wool pulled over their eyes would come sit in a circle around cattle wearing rosettes. Something that once had been simply a display of occupational skill had become a machine whose purpose was to confirm the Roman character of a simplistic aristocracy.

Louis (and even more, Myriam) would have been astonished to learn that people discoursed at length not only about their courage but about the symbolism of their courage. True, it required a lot of courage to face mettlesome cattle and pointed horns; but only the professionals had need of it. Of course, those who stood before the cattle like a locksmith at his vise – those people had an exact awareness of the dangers they were facing. Louis, though! For him it was a matter of passion, and passion leaves no room for clear-mindedness. He was paid to leap into the arena, but the truth was that he himself would have paid to do it. When he dodged the horns of an animal with a simple twist of the hips, it wasn't so as to save his liver or his spleen: it was to obey, finally, the essence of all the various bloods he bore within himself. When thunderous applause broke out, he had already been applauded for a good five minutes by the two Myriams, by Bicou, by the old man, by all the male and female Quasimodos, and maybe even the forty-franc father. When the crowds of willing dupes hoisted him on their shoulders, he had no interest in his own glory, but slept like a contented lover.

When he came out of prison, then, he saddled his horse at the house of a pal who'd been looking after it, and he went back to his delta. The place had changed a lot; the land continued its tragic life, but it was no longer used for anything but scenery. Even the sea. Even the gilded flotsam of the sea. He had a dim sense that the day would come when the great rectangle of Aigues-Mortes itself would break, like the seashells he could hear crunching in the sand under the hooves of his horse.